THE FINAL GATE

by Wesley Southard
and Lucas Mangum

Encyclopocalypse Publications
www.encyclopocalypse.com

Though we both love and adore Lucio Fulci, the authors would like to dedicate this book to his oft collaborator, screenwriter, and gore imagineer, Dardano Sacchetti. We'll keep our eyes out for you.

Seas of Darkness, Gates of Hell

Woe be unto him who opens one of the seven gateways to Hell, because through that gateway, evil will invade the world. – *The Beyond*

Known as the Godfather of Gore, director Lucio Fulci was one of Italy's biggest genre exports whose fame (and infamy) peaked in the late 1970s/early 1980s. After mostly comedy and western work in the first decade of his directorial career, he shifted to *giallo* territory with *One on Top of the Other/Perversion Story* in 1969. *Gialli* were crime thrillers that gradually became more stylish and stalk-and-murder oriented after Mario Bava's landmark *Blood and Black Lace* (1964) and Dario Argento's commercially successful *The Bird with the Crystal Plumage* in 1970. Fulci followed up the more traditional *One on Top of the Other* with the psychosexual *A Lizard in a Woman's Skin* a year later with arguably his first famous setpiece (Florinda Bolkan has a vision of eviscerated dogs dangling from hooks in a sanitarium, their internal organs still pulsing) and his *giallo* masterwork

Don't Torture a Duckling in 1972, about a child-killer in a rural Italian town. Cue his second setpiece featuring Florinda Bolkan, who is brutally beaten to death with chains by superstitious townspeople in *Duckling*. It's curious that Fulci's films took such a more violent shape than Argento's without much of a precedent—the sadistic deaths in Dario's films wouldn't become especially gory until *Deep Red* in 1975. (The irony—Argento's films were more heavily truncated in their US releases while Fulci's far gorier offerings tended to make it over here perfectly intact.)

Toward the end of the 70s, Fulci once again made an impactful genre transition after a couple westerns (including *Four of the Apocalypse*), a *giallo* (*Seven Notes in Black/The Psychic*), an Edwige Fenech comedy, and family fare like *White Fang*. The success of George Romero's *Dawn of the Dead* in 1978, a coproduction with Dario Argento released in Italy as *Zombi*, created a need for a cash-in. With no restrictions on titling a movie as if it were a sequel, Fulci's classic *Zombi 2* released in 1979. A tonally different film from *Zombi*, it held its own with some gory highlights—the infamous "eyeball" scene and the unforgettable shark versus zombie sequence, in addition to the many maulings and disembowelings that are part and parcel of any respectable undead enterprise. While the film was a hit and a staple of video stores throughout the 1980s, it was possibly most important for uniting him with his most pivotal collaborators—writer Dardano Sachetti, cinematographer Sergio Salvati, special FX artist Gino de Rossi, editor Vincenzo Tomassi, producer Fabrizio de Angelis, and composer Fabio Frizzi. Most of them (save de Angelis) would be involved a year later in my personal favorite, *City of the Living Dead/The Gates of Hell.*

In the New England town of Dunwich, the gate to Hell is opened when Father Thomas hangs himself in the cemetery. This is the only justification for the horror that follows. We never know why, other than maybe because it was foretold in the Book of Enoch, and that is the strength of it—nightmare logic. Catriona MacColl, another vital collaborator to this period of Fulci (apparently much to her chagrin) is buried prematurely and nearly has her face split with a pickaxe by her rescuer. A sense of desolation sweeps through Dunwich. There's a worm-ridden body in an abandoned house where town pariah John Morgen/Giovanni Lombardo Radici keeps his blow-up doll. Father Thomas returns to rub worm-writhing muck in one victim's face in a repulsive baptism, or simply stares on with bleeding eyes until a woman promptly vomits her digestive tract with a few bonus organs from the cardiopulmonary system. A storm of maggots blows into a house until the inhabitants can't take a step anywhere without crushing some underfoot. The pariah finds acceptance with a pneumatic drill. The undead appear throughout town, teleporting wherever someone needs their brains ripped through the tops of their skulls. An apocalyptic feel presides as Fabio Frizzi's score trudges like some rotting monstrosity. There's no logic beyond the gate being open.

One might consider said gate a "door of death," another of which opened a year later in *The Beyond/Seven Doors of Death,* considered Fulci's best by many. A warlock is the recipient of more chain justice from a mob a la *Don't Torture a Duckling* in the basement of his hotel, and crucified and drenched in burning wax. A woman reading a prophecy in the Book of Eibon over these events is spontaneously struck blind with cataract eyes. Years later, Catriona MacColl inherits the hotel and another door to death is opened. A plumber has his eyes gouged out by the warlock, who has been sealed behind the wall for decades. His widow's face is melted by acid in excruciating detail. A man investigating the architectural plans of the hotel is paralyzed in a fall and set upon by spiders that feast on his mouth and tongue. The blind woman from the prologue and her service dog Dickie are waiting for Catriona MacColl in the middle of an eerily desolate causeway. An eyeball is skewered on a spike pounded through the back of someone's head. The plumber and widow's daughter is possessed. Not to be outdone by Daniel's wolf hound from *Suspiria,* Dickie attacks and will not be confused for White Fang. The dead return at an otherwise empty morgue/hospital where the plumber/widow's daughter has enough of her skull blown off to make you wonder if Harry Callahan stood in for David Warbeck (especially since Warbeck loads his pistol through the barrel in the elevator). A door leads miles away, back to the hotel where the warlock's painting is an infinite vision of Hell. Overwhelmed by the madness and impossibility of what they are experiencing, David Warbeck and Catriona MacColl face the sea of darkness, and all therein that may be explored. Fabio Frizzi's hypnotic score lends a dreamlike eeriness to warmer, Southern gothic horrors. I had the privilege of watching *The Beyond* while Frizzi and his band performed the score live, which was an amazing way to experience a film I've enjoyed since I discovered it twenty-five years ago.

City of the Living Dead and *The Beyond* abound with as many setpieces as eye-zooms. Peripheral characters fall afoul of grotesque fates as apocalyptic doom infests entire towns. The reason of reality is lost to a fever dream of the macabre. This is not something that will resonate with everyone. If someone discusses this period of Fulci's work while sounding like an article written for *Variety,* lamenting production values or the screenplay or whatever, they just don't have the frequency for the broadcast. It's about a mood, an atmosphere, the ease with which the most shocking things occur.

The core collaborative group along with MacColl would also work on Fulci's *The House by the Cemetery,* which feels the closest tonally to *COTLD* and *The Beyond,* without actually being involving another open door of death. A family moves into a New England house where the 150-year-old undead horror Dr. Freudstein has been sustaining his rotting life with help from his victims. Notorious for the misguided dubbing of the child Bob, the film supplies some inspired setpieces of gory excess, with Fabio Frizzi's score lending a prevalent somberness to the proceedings that makes its rather hopeless ending all but inevitable. In the same year, Fulci returned to the giallo with the merciless *New York Ripper,* which like William Lustig's *Maniac* proved to be too much for the sort of fans who might have thought they'd clamor for such a film. No surprise that I love that one (and *Maniac,* for that matter), but Fulci would largely dial back the graphic content for the next few years. The otherwise quite enjoyable *giallo Murder Rock* seems tentative, victims stabbed in the heart with a needle a far cry from the intestinal vomiting, eyeball impalings, ripped-out throats, nipple excisions, and broken bottle genital stabbings of yore. Such wanton carnage prevailed even in something like his Mafia movie from 1980 (the same year as *City of the Living Dead), Contraband/The Smuggler.*

Sadly, the Italian film industry crashed toward the end of the 80s, which along with his declining health restricted him at the point when traditionally Fulci should have been making another big impact. His already minimal budgets were further restricted, and much of his later work became direct-to-video and made-for-TV films. The pendulum did at least swing back with his trademark setpieces, though, with the infamous wishboning in *Demonia* and multiple demented moments in the over-the-top *Cat in the Brain.*

Fulci never did open another door of death cinematically, but thankfully we have Wesley Southard and Lucas Mangum's *The Final Gate* to do that for us. Wesley Southard has quickly made a name for himself with such books as *The Betrayed, Closing Costs,* the Splatterpunk Award-winning novella *One for the Road* and nominated collection *Resisting Madness,* and *Cruel Summer.* Lucas has built his own following in the past five years with *Flesh and Fire, Gods of the Dark Web,* the stand-out Splatterpunk Award-nominated novellas *Saint Sadist* and *Extinction Peak,* and the collection *Engines of Ruin,* among others. They're both newer names that everyone will be seeing a lot more.

Wes has also collaborated with Somer Canon on *Slaves to Gravity,* while Lucas cowrote *Pandemonium* with me. Not unlike our exploration of the world of Lamberto Bava's *Demons* in *Pandemonium,* these two Fulci acolytes are filling the demand for the sort of story many of us Italian horror fans would have loved to have seen from the beloved Godfather of Gore, but never had the chance. You might recognize a friend or two from Lucio's oeuvre in the pages ahead, as well as the sort of deranged setpieces and cruel horrors that you would expect to see in one of his splatter epics. In such a chaotic world, you can't trust the safety of anyone or even predict who will live long enough to emerge as the true protagonist.

Those who haven't experienced the world of Fulci before need not worry, as you shouldn't be alienated from meeting the story on its own terms. You are certainly encouraged to seek out Fulci's work if you enjoy this labor of love, though. You may appreciate its origins in the maggot-dripping, brain-drilling, digestive-tract-regurgitating, eyeball-piercing world of Lucio Fulci. For now, there are nightmares on the periphery at the orphanage, and while woe may be unto him who opens one of the seven gateways, it is a pleasure to have another one to enter after so many years.

Ryan Harding
May 2021

The Final Gate

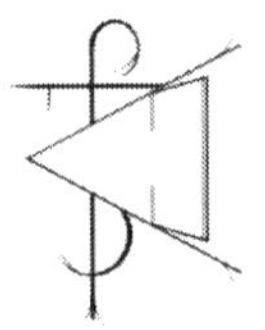

Something stirred within the room.

Terrified, Bryce swiftly rolled onto his side and pulled the covers up over his head. It was long after lights out, and he had yet to fall asleep, lying awake hours after Miss Myra had tucked him and everyone else in for the night. Ever since Jake, his roommate, had been adopted last week, nights in the corner bedroom of the west wing of the house were much lonelier—and far more terrifying. Sure, he was friends with some of the other kids, but he and Jake were as tight as brothers. He hadn't seen his actual brother, Brandon, in a long time, so Jake was the next best thing. They did everything together. Now he had nobody to talk to, nobody to laugh and carry on with. No one to share his nightly dread. The safety beneath the comforter would just have to do until they filled the empty bed across the room.

These days that wasn't a guarantee.

Even before his friend was whisked away to his new life, Bryce hated nighttime, the way the shadows closed in on him from every corner of their room. Outside, leafless tree branches danced in the midnight moon, their large, twisted hands scraping at his windows. Waving. Teasing. Desperate to taste him. He trembled. Miss Myra had once read him a poem. He couldn't recall all of it but he remembered something about the woods being dark and deep, and he would have miles to go before he closed his eyes to sleep. But those woods outside the St. Luke's were definitely *not* lovely. He never ventured past the back yard and beyond the tree line during playtime, at least not without an adult. The noises that echoed throughout the Sugar maples and oaks were best kept on the other side of a window or blanket.

The thing inside his bedroom was a whole other problem.

The floorboards creaked beneath its feet. A long, wheezy moan escaped its lips.

Bryce countered with his own pitiful whimper. He desperately wished Jake was there with him. Jake was smart. He always knew what to do! But he was alone: no friends, no parents, no one to drive the night away. Even if he screamed, how long would it take Miss Myra or Mister Lionel to come running? Could they get there in time to turn on the light and save him?

Bryce didn't think they could.

The floorboard creaked louder. Closer.

Another breathy moan.

"No..." he cried.

The blankets began to slowly drag across his body.

"No! No!"

A moment later they hit the floor. The terror building inside Bryce boiled over. He flipped over in the bed. He had to see.

A small shape stood next to him, hidden in shadows. It moaned again, louder, strained. It took another step closer.

Bryce screamed.

Jake, his best friend, his brother, stood before him in the moonlight. But it was not him at all, at least not how he remembered him. His peach skin was now sunken and sallow, streaked with dirt and splashed with bright, fresh blood. More dark red fluid bubbled over his friend's blackened, cracked lips, and several loose teeth joined the ruby cascade. Ropes of green and yellow slime dribbled from his nose and ears. His dead, milky eyes stared down at him, unblinking.

"Jake! No! It's not you! No!"

The boy took another step toward the bed, his

stiff arm reaching out.

Acting quickly, Bryce leapt with a shriek.

That wasn't his friend! That wasn't Jake!

As he scrambled off the mattress, his foot wrapped around the bedsheet. A moment later he crashed to the floor. The breath *whooshed* from his lungs, forcing him to suck in a deep, terrified cry.

Another hand extended out from underneath the bed and seized his ankle.

Nails bit deep into his skin, immediately drawing blood. Bryce screamed once more, kicking and pushing as another small, rigid body used his flailing appendage to pull itself out from the dark. The second small figure moaned, noxious black fluid dripping down her face. Panicked, Bryce kicked at the little girl with his free leg, striking her over and over in the head with his heel. Her forehead split open, and the stench of rotten sewage immediately filled the room. When Bryce finally freed his leg from her grasp, he hopped up and hobbled to the far end of the room, near the window, and pressed himself against the wall.

Jake and the little girl, who he now recognized as Allie, slowly shuffled his way. Dead eyes trained on him, they moaned in unison.

"Miss Myra! Mister Lionel!"

They were boxing Bryce in. Other than out the

window, three stories off the ground, there was no way around them.

"Miss Myra! Mis—Mister Lionel!"

Closer and closer they crept. Moaning. Bleeding. Rotting.

"M—Mommy! I want my mommy!"

He suddenly remembered the closet door not two feet to his right. He dashed for it, hoping it was a safe place to hide until an adult could save him. He ripped the door open—

—and a pair of strong hands shot out and seized his shoulders.

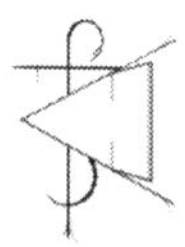

It was ten minutes before quitting time, and Robert decided to steal away for a quick smoke before his forty-five minute drive back to the city. Standing near the barn so no one could see him, no one but the goats and pigs rustling around in their pens, he let his mind wander as it always did in those few quiet minutes a day when he wasn't fixing something or cleaning up messes. Today had been an especially rough one. With two sizeable holes in the drywall to patch up, four separate toilets to unclog, and a full replacement of the industrial kitchen sink, it was a wonder he was even able to still stand the way his back was these days. But it was good work. Honest money. And he liked being around the kids, even if he was constantly fixing their unholy messes. He often watched them as he worked and reminisced about the time he was that young and free, nary a care in the world. That was long before his parent's move from New York City to Massachusetts…to that house…and that basement.

That fucking basement.

He didn't remember much of that time in his life—back when he used to go by that ridiculous old nickname his parents insisted on calling him—but the one thing his brain refused to let go of were the screams. By the time those screams had stopped, he was an orphan, just like the poor kids here at St. Luke's. It was hard life being on his own, hopping from one foster home to the next. Some were great. Others…not so much. He vowed early on to spend his life helping kids just like him, parentless and in desperate need of direction, but the further along in life he got, the more he realized it just wasn't going to happen. He couldn't afford college or get the proper schooling to be a child phycologist or doctor, so all he was left with was his hands. After years of traveling up and down the East Coast, he answered a newspaper ad for a handyman for an orphanage on the outskirts of Philadelphia. To his surprise, he was hired on the spot. He liked the kids, and they seemed to like him back. It was the people who ran the place who were…a little off. *Bunch of modern day hippies,* he thought. Not to mention these woods. They absolutely creeped him out.

A scream broke the silence.

The cigarette leapt out of his left hand, and he nearly spilled the box of Fiddle Faddle in his right. He turned to look up, his eyes scanning the blackened windows high above. He held his breath, listening. He was fairly certain he'd actually heard it, but maybe it was a TV or some of the kids screwing around. Sure, it was past their bedtime, but that didn't mean the little rascals didn't find creative ways to entertain themselves when the caretakers were asleep. *Let them play*. Those kids had nothing but the clothes on their backs and hope in their hearts, and some not even that. *Have fun while you can,* he always said. You never knew when everything you cared about could be snatched from you, just like that.

Mommy! Daddy! I'm scared!

Robert grimaced at the memory. He reached down to grab his cigarette.

Another terrified scream ripped through the house.

No mistaking that for a TV.

In an instant, Robert dropped his snack box and ran around the house to the back door. He burst into the kitchen. Like the starless sky outside, nearly every single light in the massive house was off. There were night lights plugged into the outlets in every room, but they gave very little view of where to walk without tripping. The kitchen itself was still crowded with his tools, various hammers and wrenches splayed haphazardly across the floor. He would have to get back here early to finish the sink and clean up before Lionel cooked breakfast.

His chest heaving with adrenaline, he stood there in the dark, waiting for the scream to repeat. He glanced over toward the cellar door and shivered.

Let me out!

Another scream ruptured the silence, louder and harder than before.

Unnerved, Robert raced across the kitchen, through the hallway, and into the living room, careful to swing himself around the couches and the various baskets of toys lined up against the wall. When he reached the staircase, he took the carpeted steps two at a time. From the sound of it, the screams were coming from one of the top two floors, but the distance told him it was most likely the top level, where most of the boys were kept.

The steps creaked loudly as he ran up, and with each one he wondered why no one else had woken up yet. Though Kurt, the head supervisor, lived off site, as did the St. Luke's owner, Dick Martel, the two other caretakers lived there full time. Myra's personal quarters were on the second floor, where the girls slept, and Lionel stayed on the top floor. Someone *had* to have heard the child's scream by now. Yet the third floor hallway was as dark and quiet as the rest of the house.

Robert crept toward the first door, Lionel's bedroom, and lightly rapped his knuckles on the wood. "Lionel!" he whispered. "Wake up, man. One of the kids is causing a fuss." He waited a few moments, then knocked harder. "Hey, Lionel, wake up!" He tried for the doorknob, but found it locked. "Damn it, man, someone's in trouble! Come on, this is a little out of my jurisdiction. Wake—"

The door at the end of the hallway slowly creaked open.

Robert froze, his breath catching in his throat.

It continued to swing inward, revealing the black void inside room 3-6.

Trembling, Robert swallowed then slowly inched along the hallway, watching intently as the far door yawned wide open. Not a single sound came from beyond the other closed doors. In fact, all he could hear was the rhythmic thundering of his heartbeat. When he reached room 3-6, no one was there to greet him. Who occupied that particular space? Jake? Billy? No—Bryce. The kid was all alone in there. No wonder he was scared.

"Bryce?"

He stepped into the pitch black room and reached for the light switch. Nothing happened. He tried it a few more times, silently cursing that there was yet another thing for him to now fix. He squinted, trying to make out anything in the dark. A cabinet. A dresser. Two chests filled with toys and games. And two beds. Both appeared to be empty.

"Hey, Bryce," he whispered. "Buddy, you in here?"

Much like the rest of the house, the room was void of life, and that worried him terribly. The kids should have all been in bed by now, tucked in and fast asleep. Eight PM was lights out at St. Luke's, every single night, no ifs, ands, or buts. Once each child was accounted for, the doors were shut for the night. So where the hell was this kid? He cautiously walked deeper into the room, moving past the first bed to look toward the second—

—and found a small shape huddled against the wall.

Robert ran to the young boy. "Bryce, buddy,

everything okay?"

Bryce didn't answer. Directly below the window, the child was in a sitting position, and though his body was facing the room, his upper half was turned and pressed against the wall, hiding his face.

"You okay, kiddo? Are you hurt or are you just screwing around with me?"

The boy didn't move.

"Come on, Bryce. It's too late to be playing around like this. Time to get back to bed. Don't want to anger Mister Lionel." He reached down to turn the boy's shoulder. "Let me help you—"

Bryce's upper body turned toward him.

Robert gasped.

Black and green bile oozed like sludge from the child's mouth, dripping down his chin in a thick, viscous-like soup. Robert went to meet Bryce's eyes, but there was nothing to look at. Blood wept from the empty sockets where his eyes should have been. Wet gurgles bubbled up through Bryce's throat as his small body slid down the wall and fell limp to the floor.

Robert's hand went to his mouth. "Dear Lord in Heaven…"

He was suddenly aware of someone standing next to him.

Before he could turn, something flashed in the moonlight, and a moment later it penetrated the side of his neck. Blood sprayed through the dark, gushing down his baby blue work shirt in a coppery wave. He tried to scream, but warm fluids immediately filled his throat. His eyes bulged, staring at the one who aimed to kill him. But the darkness hid his assailant perfectly, leaving only a pale hand visible as it held the embedded blade.

The hand forcefully pushed Robert backwards, the long knife still in his neck, until he collapsed onto the tiny bed behind him. The hand remained firm, keeping him in place while fresh blood continued to rush from his body. He tried to fight, to claw and kick, but he grew weaker with every passing second.

Multiple footsteps shuffled toward him in the dark. Moans echoed throughout the room. Robert lifted his head to look back—

—but several small hands greedily grasped his face. They smashed his cheeks and nose, pressing hard into his skin with cold, dead flesh.

Despite the blade lodged in this throat, Robert still managed to scream—*"Mommy! Daddy!"*—as their tiny hands dug his unworthy eyes from their sockets.

L'inferno sulla terra è qui!

A meno che non possano chiudere...

Il Cancello Finale!

(Hell on earth is here! Unless they can close...
The Final Gate!)

Scritto e diretto da

Wesley Southard e Lucas Mangum

(written and directed by Wesley Southard
and Lucas Mangum)

"Honestly, I think it's a bunch of bullshit," Brandon said, taking another shot.

The whiskey burned on the way down but cooled to a more agreeable temperature when it reached his belly. Only it didn't make him feel any better. He slammed the glass back down.

Jillian watched him closely. She took a modest sip from her porter and frowned. "You don't think he was really adopted?"

"Something just doesn't…I don't know." He shook his head. *It should've been me,* he thought miserably. He was off parole now. Working a steady job. Sober, until tonight when he'd heard the news. "The idea of my baby brother having to go live with some do-gooder strangers just pisses me right off."

Jillian took his hand across the table. "Well, if they are good people, then maybe it's what's best. Don't you think?"

"That's the thing. I don't know who they are. I don't even know where he is."

He flagged down the barmaid.

"Maybe you should slow down a little," Jillian said.

"No, if I'm gonna fall off the wagon, I may as well fall hard enough to bruise."

"And what then? I get to pick up the pieces?"

Brandon looked into Jillian's golden eyes. Her expression was soft. She cared about him a great deal. She knew all about his criminal record. His anger. His damage. But she stuck by him. Women like that were hard to come by. He sighed when the barmaid approached.

"Can I get a seltzer?" he asked.

"Sure thing," the woman said.

Jillian gave Brandon a slight smile that warmed him better than any whiskey could. He'd met her outside of an AA meeting. She wasn't an alcoholic herself. She'd been walking her dog, a wolf hybrid named Smoke, and happened to pass the church where the meetings were held just as Brandon was getting ready to leave. He'd had a lifelong fascination with wolfdogs but was never in a position to own one himself, so he immediately struck up a conversation. Despite her initial reservations about his addiction, they'd hit it off nicely. That was three years ago, and now Smoke was every bit Brandon's dog as he was hers.

"I know there's probably no way I can adopt him now. I just want to know he's okay. That's all, I guess."

Jillian looked off to the side. There was something distant about her expression, like she wasn't actually there, or she was looking at something far away.

"What is it?" Brandon asked.

"I might know a guy."

"An ex?"

She rolled her eyes.

"Okay, so, yes. What is he, a private detective or something?"

"Yeah. I don't know if he's still doing that, though. I have him blocked, but I can reach out."

"He's not weird or anything, is he? Like, you won't be uncomfortable?"

She laughed. "Weird, yes. Uncomfortable, not in the way you'd think. He wasn't abusive or anything. It just didn't work out."

"You think he will help?"

"We'd probably have to pay him."

"That's fine. You sure you're okay asking him?"

He tried to remain neutral when he asked. He didn't want her to do anything she didn't want to do, but he also desperately wanted to know that Bryce, his baby brother, was okay.

"Jillian, babe! To what do I owe this dubious

pleasure?"

The red haired, loud-mouthed guy on the video chat screen looked like no private detective Brandon had ever seen. He came off like a California surfer bro. He smiled brightly and wore a sun faded Dave Matthews Band shirt. Brandon couldn't imagine how the dude wound up investigating fraudulent insurance claims in Northeast Philadelphia.

"Dan, this is my boyfriend Brandon."

"Brandon, what's up, man? So, how long you been putting the pole to my girl?"

Brandon felt his fists clench. He wanted to demand Jillian to hang up, but if this guy was a legitimate detective, and was willing to charge a reasonable price, he supposed he could put up with a few off-color comments. *Try that shit when we're alone, punk.*

"That's none of your business," Jillian said, rolling her eyes. "And I'm not your girl anymore, so knock that crap off."

"Hey," Dan said, throwing his hands up in defense. "I'm just having a little fun. No harm in that. So, if you're not calling to catch up, what's going on?"

"We want to hire you," Brandon said.

"Hire me?"

Jillian asked, "You're still running your business, right?"

At this, he laughed. "Yeah, I'm still helping Karen's catch their schlub husbands getting handjobs from underage babysitters."

"Jesus Christ," Brandon muttered.

"I'm sorry. I'm just trying to lighten things a little. Here how's this?" Dan sat up higher in his chair and pretended to adjust an invisible necktie. He loudly cleared his throat. "How can I help you fine folks today?"

"It might be a little above your paygrade," Jillian said.

Zing, Brandon thought. He'd have to give her credit for that one later.

"Try me!" Dan countered.

She nodded at Brandon.

"I need you to help me find my brother. He was adopted from an orphanage called St. Luke's. It's just outside of Chadds Ford. I was going to adopt him, but I…well, things didn't work out."

"Couldn't get the paperwork filed in time?"

"Something like that."

"You should probably tell me."

"It's not relevant," Jillian said quickly.

Brandon sighed. "No, it's fine. I've got a record. Wasn't allowed to do shit until my parole was over." He paused. His hands were still making fists. He loosened them and flexed his fingers. "Anyway, they say he was adopted, but they won't give me any information about the new family or him or fucking anything."

"That's some shit, bro."

"Tell me about it."

Rubbing Brandon's thigh, Jillian added, "He just wants to know his little brother's okay. His parents had them several years apart, but they were very close."

"We had to be," Brandon said, but left it at that. Jillian's ex didn't need to know that after their mother died, their father had taken to drinking himself into oblivion, leaving the kids to fend for themselves until a neighbor stepped in and called CPS.

Dan nodded. "Well, I'm not going to turn down money, but you know there are proper channels to go through, right? Surely, you have some legal recourse."

Brandon tried very hard to keep a poker face and hold Dan's gaze. He could feel his jaw getting tight. He forced his eyes from drifting away. Dark things threatened to float to the surface of his subconscious.

"Come on, you know how lawyers are."

"I know how private dicks are, too," Dan said with another hearty laugh.

Jillian said, almost reluctantly, "We've…heard things about that place."

"Jill …" Brandon started.

"No, it's okay," Dan replied. "I've got an open mind. Go on."

"Let's just say that Bryce isn't the first kid to fall through the cracks," Jillian said.

"What? Are the owners, devil worshippers or something?"

"We're not sure," Brandon said.

"So, you want me to go to the *maybe* haunted orphanage in the woods and make sure your baby brother isn't bear chow or something?"

Brandon was at his breaking point, wishing the other man was here so he could strangle the dumb prick. "Yo, fuck you, man."

"I'm sorry, I'm sorry! Fucking, you know? I've got problems with my filter sometimes. That's why me and your girl didn't work out."

"Wasn't the only reason," Jillian mumbled.

Dan kissed at the camera. "You love me, and you know it."

"What are your terms?" Brandon asked through gritted teeth.

"I charge seventy dollars an hour." Brandon felt his guts clench. "But for you? I'll charge fifty. I'll work a couple hours a day and let you know what I uncover each evening. Rinse and repeat until you've found out what you want to know."

Jillian glanced at Brandon and cocked an eyebrow.

A hundred bucks a day was a lot of money for him, even with Jillian's help. It would have to be peanut butter sandwiches and roast chicken ramen for a while, but for Bryce, it was worth it. Brandon would never sleep again if he didn't know his flesh and blood was okay.

"Let's do it," he said.

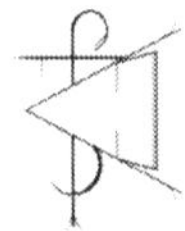

Kurt Wiser was torquing the newly-replaced P-trap under the sink in the boy's bathroom when Myra burst inside and told him they had a visitor. With a final crank, Kurt tightened the pipe and shimmied out from under the sink, trying not to think about the cold liquid soaking the back of his pants.

"How many times do I have to tell you? Fucking knock."

"Such anger!" she declared. "Kind of clashes with your hippie bullshit, don't you think?"

He sat up and wiped his hands on his legs. "Let *me* worry about my image, Myra. You should be concerned how it might look if you pop in here unannounced when one of our charges is beating his meat."

She looked him over. "No sign of Robert, huh?"

He stood and stretched his lower back. "No, there's no sign of Robert. You think I'd be lying in stray piss, fixing a sink, if there was any sign of Robert?"

"I don't suppose you would. Now, about this visitor..."

"Just give me a second to collect myself." He turned on the sink, and seconds later, water sprayed from the pipe below, pattering the floor and soaking the cuffs of his slacks. He kicked his wrench across the room. "Motherfucker!"

One of the kids, a ten-year-old ginger named Donnie, popped his head in.

"You're not supposed to say those kinds of things, Mister Kurt. You tell us not to swear all the time. Do you have an anger problem? My mom used to say..."

"Not now, Donnie."

"Why not?" the boy asked.

"Aren't you supposed to be out with the goats?" Myra suggested.

"I have to drop a deuce."

Kurt groaned and held open the bathroom stall. "Okay, fine. Just...don't use *this* sink." He pointed to the one he'd been working on.

"Okay, Mister Kurt." The kid paused halfway into the stall. "Where's Mister Robert?"

"Never you mind."

The kid entered the stall and locked it. Kurt followed Myra into the hallway.

"Okay, so, this visitor. Who are they?"

"He says he's with CPS."

"Shit," he mumbled.

"I heard that, Mister Kurt," Donnie said, then groaned as he tried to defecate.

Kurt closed his eyes and counted to three. It was a strategy he'd learned by Googling anger management. It never made him any less angry, but it sometimes prevented him from saying or doing something he'd later regret.

"Where is he?" he asked.

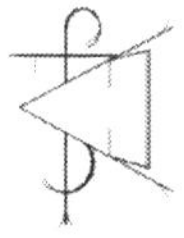

The broad-shouldered, red-haired man smiled a bit too widely when he saw Kurt and Myra coming out to meet him. He was dressed in a brown suit with a burnt orange tie. He held out a strong-looking hand when Kurt approached.

"Are you Kurt Wiser?" he asked.

"I am. Who are you?"

"Dan Sayles. I'm with Child Protective Services and I'm conducting a routine inspect—"

Kurt didn't take his hand. "You have any identification, Mr. Sayles? Can't just let every Joe off the street go poking around my business?"

"Of course, Mr. Wiser, of course." Dan Sayles produced an official-looking name badge from his breast pocket. His smile had thinned, but not much. "Satisfactory, I hope?"

"I suppose so. I guess there's no way for me to tell if it's real or not."

"We have a book in the office we can use for reference," Myra said.

"I'm sure that won't be necessary. Will it, Mr. Wiser?"

Kurt compared the photo on the card and the man before him. "No, I don't suppose it will."

Dan took the badge back and put it away. Myra narrowed her gaze at him, but Kurt took him by the elbow.

"You can come on in and have a look. One of our sinks in the boys' room is broken, but I think you'll find everything else up to snuff."

"I'm sure I will, my good man, but you know how government is. Everything has to be documented and itemized or it all falls apart."

They had a laugh at that. Even Myra cracked a smile.

"All right," Dan said. "Let's have a look around."

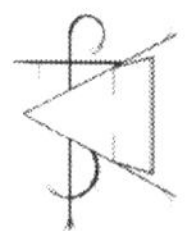

Dan followed Kurt and Myra to the fenced-in area where kids were running around with several goats. A pot-bellied pig lay sleeping in a shaded corner. A blonde girl of about seven was kneeling beside the animal, petting it. Laughter and bleating filled the air. Some of the goats had paired off and were locking horns. A tall, lean man stood watching the kids and animals play. He turned toward the approaching trio. He was gray-eyed and hard-featured, but he had a warm smile and waved his hand in greeting.

"That's Lionel," Kurt said, pointing. "He cooks for the kids and helps supervise them along with Myra here."

"Seems like a righteous dude," Dan said.

Myra cast Dan a strange look.

"You don't talk like a G-Man," she said.

Dan scrunched his face. "Gotta keep things interesting, yeah?"

"I suppose so."

"Oh, lighten up, Myra," Kurt said.

Lionel approached them and sized up Dan, his smile fading by the time he reached them. Dan was no tater-tot, but Lionel absolutely towered over him. He was someone Dan hoped he would never have to fight, not that he expected it would come to that. All he had to do was take a look around, ask to see their records, and be on his merry way. Jillian's new man, Loser McWhat's-his-name, was probably the neurotic type, and more than likely St. Luke's had valid reasons for not sharing information with him.

"He's just here to make sure things are running smoothly," Kurt explained to Lionel.

The man's smile returned. "Pleasure to meet you," He gestured to the yard. "The animals are great for the kids. Helps them get out some energy. Teaches them responsibility."

"I'm sure," Dan said. "Do they get an education? The kids, I mean?"

"That's Miss Myra's department. Speaking of which, I guess we ought to start rounding 'em up, eh, Myra?"

She gave him a curt nod and followed Lionel back to the fenced-in yard.

Someone screamed behind Dan, causing him to flinch.

A kid was running toward them, waving his arms, still screaming. His eyes were bright. His mouth made an exuberant expression.

Kurt caught him by the arm. "It's time to get ready for studies, Donnie."

"Aw, but Mister Kurt, I was...*pooping*!" he whispered, obviously embarrassed.

"And you had plenty of time to play before that," Myra said.

"*Okay*." The young boy deflated like a balloon and turned back toward the structure.

"Did you wash your hands?" Kurt asked.

The boy flashed him a puzzled look. "You said not to use the sink, Mister Kurt."

Dan snorted and barely stifled a laugh. All the adults glared at him.

Donnie frowned. "Who's he?"

"This is Mr. Sayles," Kurt said, nearly growling. "And you're making me look bad in front of him. Let's go wash your hands. Sorry, Dan. I'll be with you in a sec."

"No worries, my good man. You want to just point me to the admin office?"

Kurt and Myra exchanged a glance. *Shady motherfuckers*, Dan thought.

"Follow me," Kurt said.

Dan followed close behind as he ushered Donnie back to the structure. Behind them, Lionel and Myra gathered the others.

In the small, rather cramped closet Wiser called his personal office, Dan sat in a peeling pleather office chair in front of a rickety wooden desk. Kurt had left him to attend to Donnie. A large stack of manila file folders was neatly placed before him, which he began to rifle through. Halfway through the first kid's file, his eyes began to glaze. Tragedy could be so dull. He wondered why people couldn't just have a life as sweet as his.

He'd rented the Hyundai for the drive out to Chadds Ford. His BMW X5 would have been a dead giveaway he was no government worker. Private investigating hadn't exactly paid for his lush lifestyle. Coming from a long, and potentially incestuous, line of wealthy car dealers had afforded him that luxury. No, he just did his dicking for kicks. His clients and their fucked-up lives had a can't-look-away, car crash quality to them, like those old *Bum Fights* videos he used to watch in high school.

Then there was Brandon. Jillian's boyfriend had nobler needs, or so it appeared. Maybe there was more to the story than Brandon had let on. Maybe the car crash or bum fight would soon present itself. If not, at least he could parlay his good work into one last lay from Jillian. *Not a guarantee, but that would be pretty cool.*

He pushed away from the desk and stretched. Growing bored, he opened some of the drawers on the clapboard desk but found nothing of note. He stood and stretched, then perused the bookshelf behind him. It mostly contained dumb hippie shit about meditation, veganism, and communism.

Sounds like the only bad shit these people do to kids is make them pay higher taxes when they grow up.

Dan went to turn away, but he glimpsed another book, hidden behind the others. He reached for it, pulling the books in front of it off the shelf, and took it into his hands.

The Seven Evil Spirits.

He cracked open the thick leather tome to a page that boasted a crude sketch of a monstrous face. The illustrated fiend had a conical head, one bulging eye and one eye that was too small. The lower half of its face was no more than a shredded mass of gristle. Dan remembered something he'd once read online about a book found bound in human flesh and inked in human blood.

The door swung open. He yelped, dropping the book.

Lionel's massive frame stood in the doorway.

"Kurt wanted me to check in and make sure you had everything you needed."

Dan found his voice. "I-I'm fine."

Lionel looked over the scattered books. "What were you doing?"

"Just, uh, making sure there aren't any objectionable texts in the building. You know, nothing that will corrupt the minds of your fragile charges and such. They are the future, right?"

"And?"

"All good," Dan said. "And I'll clean up the mess."

"No need." Lionel nodded over his shoulder. "I think you should be on your way, Mister Sayles." He then stuck out his chest and made fists against his sides.

Dan remembered thinking how Lionel was someone he never wanted to spar with. This was going to blow the job, and any small chance of getting to nail Jillian again, but he was not about to get his ass kicked by Lurch.

"Yeah, man. I think you're right. I'll be on my way then."

He tried to sneak by, but Lionel caught him by the elbow. The bigger man flashed another grin that held none of its predecessor's warmth. "Have a nice day."

He released Dan's arm, and Dan scrambled toward the exit.

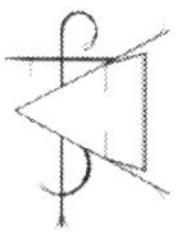

No matter what day of the week, dinner was always served at 6 PM on the dot. The rules laid out for the children were simple: you had to be inside by 5 PM, changed out of your dirty clothes by 5:15, washed up by 5:30, tomorrow's clothes laid out by 5:45, and then be in your assigned chair by five 'til. It was something the adults, especially that hard ass Mister Kurt, drilled into their brains from the moment they were taken in by St. Luke's. They may have been children now, but someday they would be adults, and before the world would accept them as societal contributors, they would need to be as 'well adjusted' as they could be, despite their abnormal upbringing. "Structure, structure, structure," Mister Kurt loved to repeat. Donnie didn't know what the hell any of that meant. Adult talk was all gibberish to him.

What he did know was that he was late to dinner. Again.

Donnie Baterman had had stomach issues for as long as he could remember. It started around the same time his parents died in that plane crash, and over the next six years it regrettably worsened. "Most likely a side effect brought on by extreme trauma or mental duress, possibly IBS..." or whatever the hell the doctors had said. Blah, blah, blah. No matter the cause, it forced him to spend far too much time squatting on a toilet, shitting his guts out. He tried to eat well (candies and sweets were strictly prohibited on the premises) and kept active outdoors like all the other kids, but at the end of the day his asshole was as permanently sore as a freshly skinned knee. Others may have brushed him off or laughed at him, but *he* didn't think it was so damn funny. Only Miss Myra was understanding. He liked her. She was definitely the nicest adult in the house.

Knowing everyone was already eating, there was unfortunately no way to sneak into dinner. He flushed and, not washing his hands, shamefully marched into the crowded dining room.

At once, everyone turned to look at Donnie.

His head down, he marched around to the other side of the large communal table and took his seat among the other children. There were fourteen all together, and not a single one was his friend. He was the oldest by at least three years, and somehow this made him the outcast.

"Hey, Donnie."

Groaning, he tried to ignore Shane, the boy sitting next to him, as he was poking Donnie in the side with his elbow. Donnie picked up his fork and pushed the buttered noodles and grilled chicken around on his plate.

"Hey, dummy, I'm talking to you."

Another couple of sharp jabs to the ribs and Donnie couldn't ignore him anymore. *"What?"*

Beneath his wild yellow mop hair, Shane grinned like a cartoon cat. "Where you been hiding?"

Donnie eyed him. "Where do you *think* I've been, bird brain? Now shut up and mind your freaking business." He turned toward the open kitchen door, where he could hear Mister Lionel washing dishes. "Mister Lionel? Could you warm up my food? It's cold!"

Woodrow, a black boy sitting directly across from him, grinned from ear to ear. "Why's your food cold, Donnie? Huh?"

Donnie frowned.

"Is it because you were busy taking another dookie?"

His face flushing hot, Donnie scanned the table.

Several of the other children had begun to giggle. Many of them were girls, which instantly made his ears burn red hot. He quickly changed the subject. "Yeah, so what? Your name's Woody. You know, like a *boner!* You're named after a wiener!"

Somehow, it didn't work. Woodrow stood up at his seat and pointed a rigid finger. "Dookie Donnie! Hey, everyone, that's Donnie's new name! Dookie Donnie!"

Donnie's jaw dropped.

Another boy, Berrshod, clapped his hands and sang. "Hey! *Dookie Donnie, sittin' on the shitter, poopin' out a log and late for his dinner!* Dookie Donnie!"

A slow chant of his new nickname swelled like a storm in the dining room. Nearly every other kid was laughing at him, their dinner now forgotten, all to be a part of his misery. Donnie glanced at the couple of empty seats at the other end of the table. Two of those spots had belonged to Jake and Bryce. He hadn't seen them in days, which meant they had probably been adopted. The only two friends he ever had would have had his back, no doubt. Tears welled in his eyes.

The only one not joining in the callous fun was Annie. Her eyes down on her plate, she absently fiddled with her peas, not paying mind to anything happening around her.

Their chanting increased, louder and louder, until Donnie felt like exploding.

Eventually, Mister Lionel stomped into the room from the kitchen. His gloved hands were covered in soap suds. "What's the meaning of this?"

When the dam behind his eyes finally broke open, Donnie shoved his chair back and dashed away. Behind him, the kids' mocking twisted into laughter as the adult told them all to calm down. But Donnie could not calm down, not at all. He ran down the hall and into the bathroom, slamming the door shut behind him.

Crouched inside the shower stall, he sobbed until his eyes burned, then vomited into the floor drain. He hated them—all of them. He hated this place and everyone in it. He wanted to go home, to sleep in his own bed, in a house with his parents…but those luxuries no longer existed. Gone in a blaze in a field outside of Allentown. This only made him cry harder.

He would get them back. All of them. Soon.

Suddenly, his stomach began to gurgle. Realizing he needed to go, he hopped onto the toilet.

The only thing that didn't exit him then was his grief.

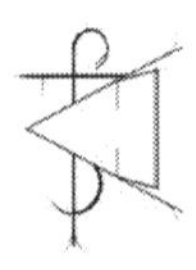

"I just don't understand any of this! Absolutely *none* of it!" Her anger swelling, Kay threw her hands up in a wild fluster.

The man across from her, Kurt Wiser or whatever the hell his name was, appeared to do his best not to lose his cool as she had, but he was starting to crumble. "Missus Lashley…why must we do this week after week?"

Kay sat up straighter in her chair across from his desk. "Because, you dumb son of a bitch, I don't like the way you speak to me or my husband. Not one little bit!" Kay could feel Fred, her husband of forty-one years, shift uncomfortably in his seat next to her. He was a good man, and she loved him almost as much as she loved her chocolate whoopie pies, but he was as timid as a church mouse, so when the going got tough, she was always the one to do most of the talking. And by God, she was going to talk. "We come in here every single week to see our granddaughter, and every time you treat us like—like we're gutter garbage."

Wiser shook his head. "Mrs. Lashley, we do no such—"

"No, I'm still speaking, you rube! I am your elder and I ask that you respect my right to speak my mind."

Sighing, Wiser nodded.

"Now, as I was *saying*, my husband and I come out here every week, which isn't easy for either of us. Bensalem may only be an hour away, but the traffic through and around the city gets worse by the year. So many young people with their concerts and their sports ball games, clogging up the streets, dancing and carrying on like hoodlums. And it goes without mention, we're no spring chickens. Mister Wiser, pile all of that on top of having to see our poor granddaughter in this prison—"

Wiser immediately spoke up. "Hey, now! This is no prison! How dare you!"

"No, how dare *you!* You goddamn hippies have stolen my granddaughter and are keeping her locked up in this retched place. When we *are* able to make it out here to visit, you rush us along, you barely let us have our time alone with her, and worst of all you won't offer us any refreshments." She smacked Fred's arm, startling him. "Tell him, dear."

Fred pursed his mustached lips. "Diabetes."

Kay continued, "You're all just so damn rude. We deserve to see our little Annie."

The man across from her sighed and ran his

hands through his short, curly afroed hair. "Kay…Fred…"

"Mister and Missus Lashley will suffice, thank you very much."

He waved. "I take extreme offence to you referring to my institution as a 'prison'. Myself, Myra, and Lionel work very, *very* hard to run a top notch, well-maintained, up-to-code, legal facility. If anything, prisons wish they were this nice. Now, you say we 'rush you along' or don't treat you fairly? The fact of the matter is, Missus Lashley, we don't have to. Your granddaughter, by the state of Pennsylvania's orders, is to remain in our care until either her father shows he can become a law-abiding citizen, or we find a suitable home that is looking to adopt."

Kay ground her dentures, making her dangling chin wobble. "You wouldn't dare!"

"I wouldn't *dare?* Ma'am, this is *my* facility, and *I* will run it as *I* see fit. It is within my legal right to keep your granddaughter under this roof, safe and secure, until a proper home is found for her. Whether that is *your* home or someone else's, remains to be seen."

"I'll—I'll sue you! The whole lot of you!"

Wiser laughed humorlessly. "Under what grounds? You have nothing to stand on, Missus Lashley." He opened his desk drawer, pulled out a thick manila folder, and dramatically dropped it on his desk top. "Of that I can assure you." He pointed to the folder. "How is your son, by the way? Edgar is his name, yes?"

Next to her, Fred let out a groan. "Please don't."

"Please don't *what?* Recount the fact your son is a felon? A drug peddler? A cocaine addict? A common thief?" Wiser sneered. "Not quite father material, I'd say."

Kay felt her chest tighten. "You leave my Edgar out of this."

Wiser nodded sarcastically. "Certainly. But how about you two? Your criminal son may have lost his privileges as a parent, but you two certainly aren't free of guilt, *are you*?" He eyed them both. "Aiding and abetting? Hiding paraphernalia? Withholding information from the authorities. Boy howdy, you two did all you could to keep your son out from behind bars."

In a whisper, Kay growled, "You know nothing about my family."

Wiser's voice rose significantly. "No, Missus Lashley, I know *everything* about your family! You think you're special? I can assure you you're not. You're just like every other dysfunctional household that forces their children to live a life not becoming of them. Those children who don't come to us out of tragedy come to us from need. A need to get away from their broken homes. From delinquent caretakers. From trusted loved ones that would lay an inappropriate hand upon them. We here at St. Luke's take in the damaged and the lost and we help bring them happiness and structure and, God willing, make them whole again.

"No, Missus Lashley you're not special. Not at all. You think you *deserve* to have your granddaughter back? That she *belongs* to you just because she's your blood? I must *strongly* disagree. I don't follow the word of lawbreakers and common miscreants. I follow the law—and that law says Annie Lee Lashley no longer belongs in your care."

Hot, embarrassing tears dripped down Kay's cheeks. "You're a goddamn monster."

Wiser frowned. "Says the monsters."

"I want to speak to your supervisor this instant!"

"*I* am in charge here, Mrs. Lashley. The only one above me is the owner, Dick Martel, and he is a very busy man who should not be bothered by the likes of you. In fact, even I can't get a hold of him most of the time."

After a few moments of silence, the bearded man settled back into his padded leather chair. He wiped his hands on his shirt. "Up to this point, you've been afforded the right to once a week supervised visitation with little Annie. After you're escorted off the premises today, I'll be making a call to Judge Harding. I believe your visits have officially come to an end, as has this meeting. Please leave now."

Kay shot up from her chair with a screech. "*You wouldn't dare!*"

Without moving his head, Wiser glared up at her. "I *said* please leave now."

"This is absolutely preposterous!" She gathered her overstuffed purse. "Fred, we're leaving, right now. By our own accord." She turned to see Fred staring at Wiser. Hate burned in his eyes. "Fred, now!"

Her husband slowly stood and walked out behind her, all while staring at the man—the monster—who had stolen their grandchild.

Outside the office, little Annie sat alone on a single wooden chair against the wall. Her eyes were glued to the floor, her small pink lips pursed in a pout.

Kay made a beeline to her. She lifted her and hugged her hard. "Oh, my baby. Oh, my sweet darling." She pulled away and forced Annie to look at her. "Don't you lose hope now, Annie. We'll figure out something. We're going to do everything we can to get you back home with us and your daddy, you understand?"

Annie's only response was a nod.

"That's a good girl. Now hug your grandpa."

Fred knelt down and embraced his granddaughter. He whispered something into her ear, and Annie nodded back to him. A kiss on her cheek and he stood with a grunt.

By the time they reached their car, Kay's anger had reached a fever pitch. "How dare he? How dare that smug little bastard think he can keep our own flesh and blood from us? How dare he think he can judge us? He knows *nothing* about us!" She turned to her husband in the driver's seat. "How can you be so calm, Frederick?"

He started the car, staring out the window with a blank expression.

"What did you tell Annie?"

Without looking, he muttered, "I've got a plan."

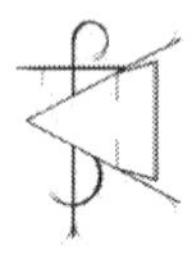

We're coming to get you. Just be ready.

Grandpa Fred's vow echoed through her brain like lyrics to a bad song. It was a song she'd heard so many times she could now sing it word for word. She'd been gifted more than her share of promises, both from her father and her grandparents, and each one was as empty as the heart space reserved for caring. The last time she'd seen her father was in court, when she was being dragged away from his embrace, and he'd said something very similar. But she didn't care. In the public eye, he was all emotion and theatrics. Behind closed doors...she was merely another thing to pawn off for more drugs. They were all as fake as the 'care' half of 'caretakers.' Sure, everyone here seemed nice enough, but they were paid to be.

At nine years old, Annie was already quite the cynic.

Yet there was something about Grandpa Fred's words that bothered her. Maybe it was the argument he and Grandma Kay had with Mister Kurt in his office, or maybe it was them being told they would no longer see her, but this time his words seemed to carry more weight. And that's what scared her. She had no idea what they had planned, but one thing she did know was she had no desire to return home. *They* may have treated her okay, but her father was still there…

"I won't go back," she whispered.

Across the room, Miss Myra was tucking Annie's roommate, Edna, into her bed. After wishing her goodnight, the woman strode over to Annie's bedside. "Did you say something, dear?"

Annie shook her head. "No, ma'am."

"Are you sure, hon? It's okay if you did. You know you can talk to me, right?"

Biting her lip, Annie nodded.

Miss Myra frowned. "Hon, what's the matter?"

She turned away as she started to cry.

"Oh, hon." The woman sat on the corner of the bed and took Annie's hand in her own, squeezing gently. "It's okay. If you have to cry, then cry it all out. Better out than in."

A minute passed before Annie could stop herself from weeping. She wiped her eyes with her blanket and sighed.

The woman asked, "You want to talk about it?"

Looking away, Annie shrugged.

"Is this maybe about your grandparents?"

She shrugged again.

Miss Myra nodded. "Mister Kurt told me about what happened today. It's all very unfortunate. I'm so sorry you had to hear all of that, hon."

Annie pulled the blanket up over her face.

"You know this isn't your fault, right? Absolutely *none* of this is your fault. You're a good girl. Your family loves you and they want to take you home, but they have to play by the rules and do it the right way. I'm sure your daddy is dying to see you again, don't you think?"

A shiver ran down Annie's spine.

Miss Myra pulled the blanket back down. "Don't you want to see them again?"

She shook her head no.

The woman nodded and considered this. "Well, I can tell you this. You're a wonderful kid, and no matter what happens, no matter where you end up, that family will be so very lucky to have you. I'd have half a mind to take you in myself."

A smile broke across Annie's lips. "Thank you."

"You're very welcome, my dear." She tapped her chin. "You know what? I've got an idea. Something fun that might cheer you up. You want to try it?"

Annie nodded enthusiastically.

Miss Myra stood. "Great! Okay, I need you to flip over on your stomach and pull up the back of your shirt." After Annie did, the woman pulled the blanket down all the way and sat back on the bed. "I don't know if I ever told you, but my family is of Scottish heritage. My grandmother, Colina, came all the way over from Scotland many years ago with her family, and they brought many of their traditions with them. One of them was this game she used to play with me when I was your age. It's called Dot, Dot, Line, Line. It used to help me calm down and relax me when I wanted to go to sleep. You ready?"

"Yes," Annie said.

"Okay, here we go." Miss Myra touched her bare back with her index fingers twice, then drew two diagonal lines. "Dot, Dot, Line, Line—" Her finger spider-walked up her back to her neck. "—let a sheep crawl up your spine."

Annie giggled, the fingers tickling her.

The woman put a fist on top of Annie's head. "Crack an egg on your head—" Her other hand hit her fist, then her fingers ran down the sides of Annie's face. "—and let it dribble onto your bed." Her fingers clutched Annie's sides. "Tight squeeze—" Then she blew on the back of her neck. "—cool breeze." She capped it off by lightly running her finger tips up Annie's back. "Now you've got the shiverees."

Her woes temporarily forgotten, Annie giggled at the rhymes and touches. Surprisingly, she now felt completely relaxed, her body sinking into the mattress. "I liked that."

"Good! Me, too."

"Good night, Miss Myra. Thank you."

The woman pulled Annie's shirt back down and the blanket back up. "My pleasure, hon. Get some rest."

Within moments, Annie was fast asleep.

When Annie awoke the next morning, her roommate, Edna, was gone.

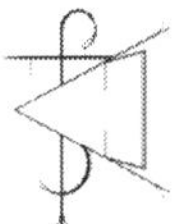

"I didn't find a whole hell of a lot, but yo, those people are shady as fuck," Dan said.

The three of them were sitting in a diner called Marion's, located off Roosevelt Boulevard on the northeast side of Philadelphia. Brandon and Jillian were sharing nachos, while Dan poked at a country fried steak that Brandon thought smelled like feet. They all had steaming coffees in front of them. A breezy Billy Joel song played over the diner's sound system.

"I knew there was something up with them," Brandon said.

Jillian asked, "What *did* you find?"

Dan chewed and then swallowed. "Like I said, not a lot. They definitely act like they've got something to hide though. And…" He frowned, considering something. He absently stirred a puddle of country gravy with his fork. From what Brandon had seen and Jillian had said, this unease wasn't common for Dan. He was a loud, confident type, easygoing and not much of a thinker, but Brandon thought he seemed perturbed about something.

"What is it?" Brandon probed.

Dan waved his hand dismissively. "Ah, nothing. They're just secretive. Like I said. I guess."

"If there's something you aren't telling us…"

"Brandon," Jillian said, putting a calming hand on his forearm.

"Look, I can go back there, if you'd like," Dan said. "I just need to try another way."

"What happened?"

The song changed from Billy Joel to a downtempo number from Bruce Springsteen. Dan told them how he'd been asked to leave by some guy named Lionel while he was checking around the office. "They didn't mind me looking at the records, but man, they really minded me snooping in their bookshelf."

"That's so strange," Jillian said.

"Not if what we heard about the place is true," Brandon muttered.

"I'm sure they're just rumors."

Dan said nothing. He couldn't meet their gazes.

"You're going back, right?" Brandon asked.

Dan looked out the window, and Brandon followed his gaze. A man dressed in gray rags carried a sign that said Jesus was coming. He had a wild look about him. The word *rabid* came to mind. Brandon knew that look. He'd had that look once upon a time. But then he'd gotten clean.

Still not soon enough to save Bryce.

"Right?" he insisted.

Dan broke his stupor and nodded. "Since they kicked me out, I'll need to get creative. It'll cost a little extra."

"Dan, no," Jillian groaned. "Come on. We agreed."

"I know, but I might have to break in. Do some illegal shit. I can't take that risk unless it's worth my while. Got a business to run, sweetheart."

"I don't believe this shit," Brandon said.

Dan glared at him, then softened and looked at Jillian. "Of course, we could come to some kind of agreement." He reached for her hand across the table.

"What the fuck, man?" Brandon took his coffee mug and hurled its scalding contents at Dan's face. The other man screamed in pain. Both men scrambled out of their booths and into each other's face. The other restaurant patrons turned to watch.

Dan scowled, "You want to try something when

I'm not sitting down, you little bitch?"

"Touch my girl again, I'll fucking kill you," Brandon hissed through his teeth.

Jillian stood and grabbed Brandon by the elbow. "Let's go. This isn't accomplishing anything."

"What did you see that got you in trouble?" Brandon asked, his voice low.

"Your punk ass is never finding out."

Jillian gave Brandon's arm a tug. "Let's *go.*"

"Better listen to what my girl says."

Brandon stared into the dark brown eyes of the man in front of him. Droplets of coffee streamed from his pale cheeks like dark tears. He wore a cocky smile. *My* girl, he'd said. Brandon saw himself rearing back and punching the fucker in the mouth with all the strength he could manage. He wanted to strike him almost more than anything in the world, but nowhere close to how badly he wanted to learn what happened to Bryce. If he kicked Dan's ass now, he'd land himself in trouble again, and he might never learn what happened.

Brandon took a seething breath and let Jillian led him out of the diner.

"We'll find another way," she said when they reached the door. "I promise."

"Yeah," he said. "Yeah, we'll see."

As they walked to her car, he began formulating

a plan of his own. It was an ugly plan, but it would be worth the risk if it worked. He just couldn't tell her.

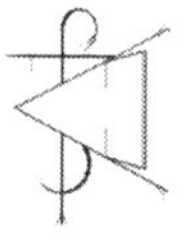

"I think I'm gonna go for a drive."

The blankets ruffled as Jillian propped herself up on her elbow. In the dark, her features were hard to read. Brandon hoped his were just as indecipherable.

"Can't sleep," he said, clarifying.

"Are you going to a bar?"

She kept her tone neutral, but he knew her well enough by now to know that she'd be disappointed if he answered in the affirmative. She'd gone with him willingly when they found out Bryce had been adopted, allowed him that one backslide into old, destructive habits. Temporary blunting of pain was the only coping mechanism he really knew. But she'd made it *very* clear that had been a one-time thing. They needed to find better ways to deal with things that hurt if he was to ever fully recover. She'd promised him she would be there to catch him if he fell. He wanted to believe her, just as he wanted to believe when she'd said earlier they'd find another way to locate Bryce. While he believed her in the former scenario, he did not trust her in the latter. It wasn't a matter of thinking she didn't care. It was more because she simply didn't understand the situation. It was a desperate one, and she didn't exactly strike him as ever being desperate. Unless there was something from her past that she hadn't told him, she had nothing in her experience to match his circumstances with Bryce.

He wanted to answer truthfully. *Yes, I'm going to a bar*. Though she'd be upset, a relapse was, for the most part, forgivable. What he *actually* aimed to do might not be. Still, he thought it best to tell her as little as possible.

Are you going to a bar?

"No, of course not," he finally answered.

"Just a drive?"

Shit. This would be harder to answer. He'd have to lie. He'd hoped to avoid that, being much more comfortable omitting truth than speaking dishonestly, especially to her. But still, some things were more important than honesty. Besides, she knew how much Bryce meant to him. In the long run, she would understand. He hoped.

"Just a drive."

She was quiet for a while, and he worried she didn't believe him. He almost told her his plan right then, came clean with her and even allowed himself to entertain a fantasy of her lending a hand, but he knew she'd talk him out of it, so he stayed quiet.

"Just be safe." She reached up to hug him.

"I will," he said, returning her embrace.

He pulled on his jeans and his favorite red Phillies T-shirt and walked out to his car. Once inside, he typed **ST. LUKE'S CHADDS FORD** into the navigation app on his phone and mounted the phone on the dashboard. He drove without any music.

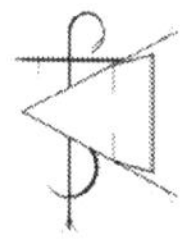

Dan Sayles couldn't sleep. He hadn't slept since his trip to that damn orphanage, and he wasn't the type of guy to lose shuteye over much of anything. Trouble was that every time he closed his eyes, he saw that awful face from the book he'd found. *The Seven Evil Spirits.*

Truly awful stuff. Vile. Satanic.

Not that he believed in that sort of nonsense.

Still...bad vibes were bad vibes, and he had them in spades.

He rolled onto his side, tucking an extra pillow between his knees. He made himself close his eyes and tried to think of anything positive. A perfect picture of Jillian was conjured, wrapping that tight body of hers around him again. She probably never would, but no big deal. Anything to get his mind off that face. He felt himself drifting and sighed with relief. Then, her face changed. *No.* The bottom third of it shredded like ground meat. Glistened red. One eye bulged. The other eye shrank. They shifted across her face, settling into unnatural places. He got the sense he was falling right before his eyes snapped open. He gasped and cursed. Shivering, he got out of bed and stumbled to the fridge.

He took out a tallboy of Pabst and downed most of it in one pull. When he finished, he immediately started on another.

Brandon made sure to cut the headlights before turning into the long gravel drive leading up to St. Luke's. He slowed the car to a creep. The field surrounding the compound was perfectly dark. Clouds obstructed the moon and stars. Much to his dismay, he forgot to bring a flashlight, but he could use his phone if necessary. He preferred to let his eyes adjust. No sense in drawing unnecessary attention.

He parked halfway up the drive and opened his door. He waited until the pitch darkness lightened to shades of gray. After getting out, he put on his thin coat and eased the door shut, so as not to be heard.

Somewhere nearby a sheep bleated.

He zipped up his dark coat, stuffed his hands in his pockets and lowered his head. If the moon ever did break through the cloud cover, he didn't want to risk it reflecting off his skin. He could allow nothing to give him away.

As expected, all of the interior lights were out as he rounded the main building. All the kids had been put to bed hours ago. The adults, whoever they were, had more than likely turned in by now, too. Still, his pulse thudded angrily. An anxious voice urged him to go back to the car and drive right the fuck home. Forget about this awful idea.

You've come too far, it said. All that recovery from his old life, from the drinking and all the awful baggage that had come along with it.

But there was another voice and it sounded much truer. All that repairing and recovery, he'd done it for Bryce. Bryce, who had been taken from him. Bryce, who he worried he may never see again.

He was just going to break into the main office, check the records, and find out where Bryce had been taken. That's all, and then he could check up on his little brother. If Bryce was in a good home, then life could go on as normal. If not, well, he'd cross that bridge when he came to it.

He approached the window to the small main office where that huckster Kurt Wiser kept all the records and files. From his back pocket, he produced a small glass cutter and cut a circle in the window just above the lock. Wiser had never installed an alarm system, this he knew ahead of time. It was something Brandon had noticed the last time he'd visited his little brother, when he'd learned the clock was really ticking. Desperate thoughts had crossed his mind.

He unlocked the window and lifted it open. Carefully, he shimmied through and took out his phone, which he'd silenced. There were several messages and missed calls from Jillian, asking where he was and when he'd be back. He felt a pang of regret but reminded himself to stay strong. He'd be out of here soon. Switching on the flashlight feature, he approached the file drawers and began to rifle through the folders. When he found the one with Bryce's name on it, he took it out and opened it on top of the desk.

When he first saw the dark spot in the center of the page, he thought perhaps that he'd put the folder down in a previously unseen puddle of something spilled. But then the edges began to glow, producing a bright orange ring. By the time he realized the papers had caught fire, the flames had blossomed like a rose.

Brandon didn't know how it happened or where the fire had come from. He only saw it form in a matter of seconds before flashing so bright it blinded him. He cried out and backed away from the growing blaze. Unexpectedly, everything went dark.

His sight was gone.

"No!" he yelled. "No, God!"

He backed into a desk chair and spilled to his ass. The chair clattered somewhere nearby. The smell of burnt paper choked the air around him, but the warmth from the flames had died down. It was suddenly very cold in the small office.

He kept telling himself that his sight would return, that it was just a temporary flash and his eyes would readjust. When they did, he would leave. *Point fucking taken.* He didn't need to be snooping. He had to cut his losses, no matter how badly it hurt. He had a whole other life to live. With his sobriety. With Jillian.

But the darkness never broke. The chill in the air became raw and biting, even through his coat.

Warm, moist breath fell against his ear.

Something had come so close to him without

hearing its approach.

"Hello, big brother."

Brandon opened his mouth to scream, but before he could expel a single note, something small but very strong punched inside and took hold of his tongue. There was a sound like the splitting of waterlogged wood, and a moment later a pain more intense than he ever imagined as his tongue ripped free from its base.

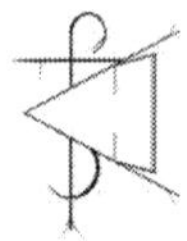

While the other children played with one another in the fenced-in back yard, Annie hid herself away inside the livestock pens. It wasn't her normal scheduled day to help clean and feed the pigs and sheep, but she politely offered to take the spot from Gene and Andy. Both equally hated being near the animals or getting dirty, so they were enthusiastic and grateful for the day off. She was happy for the time alone.

Even before being placed in the care of St. Luke's, Annie Lashley was a fierce loner. She had very few friends, normally making it a priority to keep to herself. Other kids were mostly friendly to her, but the niceties were often not reciprocated. It was all by design. She hated being that way. Annie craved companionship. But there was always one big roadblock preventing it.

Daddy.

Edgar Lashley was not a nice man, and it didn't take her long to see the distinction between right and wrong. He wasn't like all the other daddies. When he wasn't snorting, smoking, or shooting up drugs in front of her, he was throwing wild parties in the basement of grandma and grandpa's house, where she and daddy lived. She didn't like his friends or the way they looked at her…or the things they said about her when they thought she wasn't listening. But that was only when he was around. Daddy was often in jail or in court, both of which her grandparents somehow kept him out of for very long.

She hated all of them.

No matter what Grandpa Fred had told her, she would never go back. No sir.

After brushing the sheep and feeding both them and the pigs, she placed the pellet bucket aside and stepped toward the fence. She stared out into the sunlit yard. Other than the few children tending to the garden with Mister Lionel, picking fresh green beans and tomatoes for tonight's dinner, there was so much playful chaos. Kids playing tag and shooting hoops on the basketball court. Yelling and laughing. Smiles so big they nearly split their faces in two. Jealousy washed over her. Now that Edna had been adopted, she was all alone.

Edna.

Darkness clouded her thoughts. One day her roommate was there, then the next morning she was gone. She may have been young, but Annie wasn't stupid by any stretch. She'd been at St. Luke's for nearly eight months, and, as far as she could tell, no one was adopted in the middle of the night. Mister Kurt had told her Edna was officially signed out as of this morning and anything beyond that was 'not her concern.'

Annie strongly disagreed.

After speaking to that jerk Mister Kurt, she had stepped outside in a huff to walk along the fence…and discovered something that deeply bothered her. While St. Luke's was adamant about recycling, they burned most of their trash in a fire pit on the far side of the house. Whatever was left was scooped into the metal barrel and left curbside for disposal. As she picked dandelions to clear her thoughts, she had noticed something was off about the ash barrel. The lid on the overflowing container was barely holding onto the rim, and beneath it was something bright yellow. After checking to see if anyone was watching,

Annie approached the barrel and lifted the lid. Beneath it was half of a burned-up toy.

Edna's stuffed animal.

She knew what it was the moment she saw it. Edna was a few years younger than Annie and had brought in Tommy the Duck with her when her parent's died. It was all she had left in the world and now it was destroyed, ready to be tossed out and forgotten. There was no way Edna had left here without it. No way, no how. She went back inside and told no one what she saw.

Now, hours later, it festered inside her head like rotten garbage. Other than the occasional visitor and the three caretakers, two of which lived there full time, she never saw any other adults come or go. The fact was kids were disappearing overnight. And there were noises all throughout the night. Shuffling. Moaning. She may not ever want to go back home, but deep down she knew she couldn't be here for much longer.

Something caught her eye.

She stepped closer to the fence and leaned over the top board. There was movement past the low property fence, where the back lawn met the woods. Something stirred between the trees. Annie squinted. It shambled out of sight.

By Mister Kurt's rules, no one was allowed

outside of the property. Yet someone was out there. She wondered who?

The shape reappeared, standing next to a thick oak tree.

Annie held her breath—

It turned toward her. It looked like…

—gasped—

Something went *splat* against her back.

—then screamed.

A raucous round of laughter exploded behind her. Annie quickly spun around.

"Little orphan Annie, poop on her back! Runnin' down her shirt and into her crack!"

At some point, Shane, Woodrow, and Berrshod had snuck into the pen and hurled—*Oh God!*—pig poop on her. She twisted around her shirt to look. It was indeed running down her back and onto her pants, wet and cold. The smell was unbearable. The three boys cackled and high-fived. Tears welled in Annie's eyes. This place was pure hell.

"Miss Myra!"

Annie turned back to the yard and found Donnie standing outside the pen, his hands cupped around his mouth.

"Miss Myra!" he yelled again.

From out of the back door, Miss Myra stepped outside, frowning. She followed Donnie's outstretched arm right to Annie, who was crying. "What's going on out here? What happened?"

Donnie ran toward the adult. "Those dicks threw pig poop on Annie, and now she's crying."

"Watch your language, young man." She turned back to Annie, who was wiping away her tears. "Is that what transpired?"

Below her, Donnie nodded enthusiastically.

"Well then." She pointed. "You three! Inside and into your rooms now! You're all banned from this afternoon's activities."

The three boys groaned in anger and trudged past Annie and out of the pen. Shane shot an angry look at Donnie before they disappeared into the house.

Miss Myra looked down at the boy. "Thank you, Donnie. Now go play. You've got thirty more minutes."

"Yes, Miss Myra." He turned toward Annie, offering her a sad smile, before loping off toward the other children.

"Annie, honey, come here."

Shaking with anger, Annie exited the pen and marched toward the woman. The cold slop continued to drip down her back.

She put her hands on Annie's shoulders. "You okay, sweetie?"

Annie couldn't meet her eyes.

"You'll be fine. Go in and change your shirt and get cleaned up. Do you remember Mister Frizzi? He's coming by today to play some music for you all. You like his music, don't you?"

Annie could only answer with a shrug. Sighing, Miss Myra patted her shoulder, then urged her toward the door. Before stepping inside, Annie fired one last look toward the woods.

The shape that looked like Edna was gone.

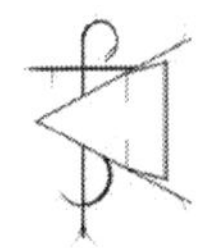

After the short concert in the living room with the old man with white hair, Donnie spent the rest of the afternoon doing his best to avoid the other three boys. He hadn't actually seen them, seeing as how they were all relegated to their rooms as punishment, but he could imagine their anger was growing by the second. The longer the day grew, the more he started to worry about what they were planning to do to him. He grew more nervous as he rounded every corner of the house, expecting them to be waiting for him. Thankfully, they remained stowed away.

All this free time gave him an idea.

While most of the kids had settled in around the house, either playing in their rooms or finger painting at the dining room table, Donnie snatched a plastic cup from the trash and carefully snuck back outside. After making sure the coast was clear of adults, he crept to the pig pen and got to work. He searched and searched, trying to find the perfect specimens. Near the back of the pen, he found them. With a tissue and a grin, he found the driest pieces of pig poop and placed them in his cup.

Shane, Woody, and Berrshod were bullies, plain and simple. Their little gang picked on just about everyone in the house, and the adults did little about it. The boys had given Donnie hell since the day he'd walked in, making his little bowel issue a house-wide joke. He'd brushed them off the first few times, laughing along with good nature, but when they got the whole brigade of kids pointing, all he could do was hide in shame. A bad haircut? Sure, that's easy to snicker at. A quick fix. Internal body issues? Stuff like that can't be helped. It drove him crazy! But when they threw that pig poop on poor Annie? That was the last straw.

They liked to talk about poop so much? Maybe they'd like to eat some?

Every day at 3pm, the children were given a healthy snack. Mister Lionel homemade all of their food from scratch, and today, much like every Thursday afternoon, it was granola day.

As quietly as he could, Donnie stepped back into the house. When the kitchen cleared of activity, he snuck in, closed the kitchen door, and strode toward the large wooden island in the center of the floor. Sitting on a metal tray were nearly a dozen or so small plastic, see-through cups full of oats and nuts. Each one had someone's name written across the front in black marker. He located the three jerk's cups and moved theirs to the front. The next part would be tricky…and gross. Grimacing, he reached bare-handed into his cup and retracted a dried hunk of pig poop. The smell was mostly gone, but it was still feces and still horribly disgusting. Using both hands, he crumpled the turd into petite, pebble-sized pieces. Once they were small enough, Donnie distributed them amongst the three cups. He used his finger to mix the contents.

The kitchen door swung open behind him.

Stifling a shriek, Donnie spun around and froze.

A man he had never seen before stood in the doorway. He was tall and lean, his hair and beard as black as a windowless room. He wore blue overalls and a red headband, and carried a clipboard.

They both stared at one another in silence.

Heart hammering, Donnie watched as the man

took a few leisurely steps into the kitchen. His eyes never left him. The closer the man got, the bigger he appeared, towering over him like a fleshy skyscraper. Donnie's knees began to shake.

The man eyed the cups, then looked back to Donnie. "Question."

I've been caught! Donnie swallowed, waited.

"Where's the trash can?"

A nervous sigh escaped Donnie's lips. He pointed a dirty, shaking finger to the cabinet next to him.

Nodding, the man leaned past him and pulled the door open. He ripped a piece of paper from his clipboard, balled it up, and threw it away in the bin.

From out of the hallway, Mister Kurt and Mister Lionel stomped purposefully into the kitchen. Mister Kurt was red-faced and angry. His curly hair and beard was glistening with sweat. "I just don't understand how this could happen!"

Mister Lionel shrugged. "Angry parents…thieves…restless teenagers. Take your pick. People have no respect for the law these days."

The other adult shook his head. "Unbelievable—*just unbelievable!* We don't have that much in the budget to be replacing windows or doors or whatever else someone wants to break. Could have been one of the kids?"

"No. The office is locked every night. You know that."

He rubbed his temples. "Was anything missing?"

Mister Lionel shook his head. "Not that I'm aware of, no. Everything appeared in order."

"Any signs of the intruder or where they went?"

"Nope. They must have given up and left."

They both turned toward Donnie, who was still frozen in place. Mister Kurt nodded at him. "Donald. How are we this afternoon?"

Donnie licked his dry lips. "Fine, sir."

"Just *fine*?"

"I'm very good, sir."

Mister Kurt's lips curled in a tight smile. "That's more like it, kiddo. A happy soul is a healthy soul. Why aren't you playing with the other children?"

Donnie eyed the cup in his hand, the one filled with pig poop, and slowly put it behind his back. "Just…just getting my snack, sir."

Mister Kurt glanced at the island. "Granola. Full of fiber and nutrients. Very good for you. Eating better sustenance like that might help your little *problem*, don't you think?"

His face growing red hot, Donnie could only nod.

The tall man handed Mister Kurt a paper from

his clipboard. "Here's your bill."

The other two adults glanced at the paper. "Jesus…" Mister Kurt moaned.

Mister Lionel shook his head. "That's how much windows cost these days? Too bad Robert's not around anymore. He could have done this for a quarter of the cost."

"Not much I can do, gentlemen," the tall man mumbled. "The company sets the prices, not me."

Frowning, Mister Kurt eyed the man. "That's fine, I suppose. The work's already been completed. Dick will have to be notified immediately."

"Let me get in touch with Mr. Martel," Mr. Lionel quickly said. "You've got more important things to worry about."

Mister Kurt nodded. "Very well."

The tall man added, "We also sell and install security systems, if you're interested."

"Are they as expensive as a new window?"

"They're louder than a new window."

Mister Kurt pursed his lips and sighed. "Let's talk business."

Nodding, the tall man led the other two toward the back door and stepped outside. When the door closed behind them, Donnie let out a long sigh of relief. *Holy moly, that was close!* Knowing he had very little time before someone else would interrupt, he swiftly added the rest of the pig poop to the boy's cups and mixed them up with his finger. He threw away the cup, wiped his hands on a towel, and hustled toward the open kitchen door—

—only to discover the three boys heading his way.

Panicked, he quickly backed away and searched for a way out. He couldn't go for the back door, as the adults were still out there. The cabinets? No, too small. The windows? Too high.

He glanced toward the basement door.

As far as he knew, the basement was off limits to all the children. In fact, he'd never even seen any adults go in or out either. The framed sign next to the door specifically stated: **DO NOT ENTRY**. Out of options, he dashed toward the door. He expected it to be locked, but the door swung open with no resistance. He stepped inside and closed it most of the way, leaving only a small crack for him to look through. A moment later, all three boys entered the kitchen with chuckles.

"I mean, you *did* see her face, right?" Berrshod said. "It was like—" He opened his eyes and mouth wide and wagged his tongue, mimicking Annie's shock.

Shane giggled, "She never saw it coming!"

Woody smacked his hands together. "Splat goes

the dynamite!"

Shane's smile died. "Yeah, and it would have been perfect if that jerk Donnie hadn't ruined it."

"Stupid Dookie Donnie," Berrshod mumbled.

"Next time we find him alone," Shane smacked his fist into his palm, "we'll show that turd a thing or two."

"Yeah," the other two agreed.

Shane reached up and found his cup of granola, as did Woody and Berrshod.

Donnie's heart thumped hard in his chest. *Eat up, ladies.* But none of the three made a move to consume.

"Maybe we could hold him down," Woody mused with a grin, "and kick him in the legs."

Shane pointed. "Yeah! Then all he could *do* is sit on the crapper and not get up."

Berrshod shook his granola cup. "That *is* his favorite thing!"

The three giggled amongst themselves while Donnie's face turned beet red in the dark. He'd like to see them try something like that. He'd fight them all. Though he balled his fists, he felt his eyes well up with tears. Why was everyone so damn mean to him?

"Let's go back to that game of Monopoly," Shane suggested. "I'm ready to bankrupt you all."

Woody nodded enthusiastically. "Yeah right!

We *all* know I'm going to beat you both."

While those two walked from the kitchen, Berrshod lagged behind. He shook his granola cup, eyeing its contents. Donnie leaned closer to the crack in the door. Berrshod then lifted the cup and dropped some of its contents into his mouth and chewed. Behind the door, Donnie threw a hand over his mouth, stifling a laugh. Berrshod chewed for a moment, then stopped. He glanced down into his cup with a confused frown. Donnie stopped laughing. He was sure the boy would find the secret ingredient. But he didn't. Berrshod shrugged and walked out of the kitchen, leaving Donnie alone once more.

Yes! Yes! Yes!

Maybe they would find out, maybe not, but holy crap that was worth it!

Donnie was about to step back into the kitchen, but something stopped him.

A noise. Somewhere below in the dark. He stood at the top of the steps, holding his breath. A few moments later the noise repeated. Something like…feet shuffling.

"Hello?" he whispered.

He went for the door again, but the shuffling repeated.

Wide-eyed, Donnie turned back to the steps and stared down into the black mouth of the basement.

"Wh-who's down there?"

The noise had now stopped.

He had no reason to be scared, but something told him to leave and not look back. No one was allowed in the basement, and as far as he knew no one had attempted the trip down the narrow, rickety wooden steps to explore. But maybe...*he* could be the first one? Suppose he found something cool? Something show-off worthy? He imagined himself displaying that item, and every kid at St. Luke's wanting to be his friend. No more Dookie Donnie! He grinned.

The wooden planks creaked softly as he descended each stair. He kept his hands out, feeling for a light switch. There didn't appear to be one. Oh well. The dark didn't bother him too much anyways. When he reached the bottom, he stood in place and let his eyes adjust to the inky dark.

When they finally did, he let out a piercing scream.

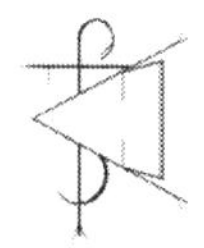

Edgar Willem Lashley was not one to suffer fools gladly. For as long as he could remember, he was a straight shooter. Not one to mince words or lie down willingly. In other words, he didn't take shit from anyone. It was he who dealt the verbal and, more often than not, physical punishment to anyone who crossed him. If you grew up in Philadelphia or any of the surrounding shithole towns, running the streets meant you instinctively developed an 'I don't fuck with you, you don't fuck with me' attitude. Sure, if people were smart, they would stay the hell out of his way, but that was Philly in the mid-1980s, where every coke-head burn-out stumbling out of a bar was looking to throw down. At forty-six, Edgar still proudly displayed those scars, like sports trophies on a mantle.

But there was still plenty of space for more.

As he drove through the country outside of the city, he intended to add a few extra...especially if anyone got between him and his baby girl. No matter what he did in his past—and he'd done some *heinous* shit—they had no right to take his only child from him. He was her parent, and despite not always being there for her, that didn't make him any less of a father. Edgar wasn't necessarily looking for blood tonight—in fact, he preferred not to hurt anyone at all—but he imagined they wouldn't happily hand Annie over to him without a struggle. He was ready. But his parents, on the other hand...

Beside him in the truck, Fred and Kay bickered like the old married couple they were. Though they both came to him with the idea of breaking Annie free, his mother seemed to have grown cold feet once the plan went from words to action.

"Fred," she cried, "this is absolutely crazy! We can't just break in and take her!"

His father shook his head. "And why the hell not?"

"Because it's absurd!"

"What happened to you? Yesterday you were all gung-ho, ready to storm the castle and rescue the princess. Cold feet got you, woman?"

Kay wiped her eyes. "Cold feet, doubt, growing a conscience—call it what you will, but this is the dumbest idea from a man who's had *a lot* of dumb ideas."

"Damn it, Kay, you said it yourself. Our little Annie deserves to be with her family, not the state or those fucking hippies running that dirty little institution. We don't know what they're doing to them there. For all we know they could be touching them."

"Don't you say that!" she yelled, wiping her eyes. "That's terrible."

Fred's voice rose with hers. "They could be doing anything with those kids! That's why we've got to bust her out."

"And what then, old man? *Hmmm?* We can't just take her back to the house. The police will be after us right quick."

"That's exactly why we're taking her to the cabin."

"The *cabin*? That's—that's five hours away! We're never going to make it all the way there!"

Fred yelled, "We've got to try something, goddamn it! We can't just leave her there!"

Kay grabbed her husband's shirt sleeve and tugged. "Please, Fred, this is ridiculous. Let's just go home—"

Edgar had had enough. *"Shut up, shut up, shut up!"* He emphasized each word by smacking the dashboard with his palm.

His parents immediately stopped arguing and stared at him blankly.

"You two listen to me *very* fucking carefully," he growled. "We are *not* going into that house guns ablaze. We go in quietly, we get my daughter, and we leave just as quietly. Got it? No gunfire, no knives. Violence is a last resort tonight. No exceptions. Nothing, and I mean *nothing*, is going to stop me from taking my daughter back." He turned to face Kay. "You hear me, ma?"

Tears welled in her eyes.

"I asked you a fucking question!"

She flinched, then nodded.

"Good, because I'd hate to kick your fat ass out of this truck and leave you to the bears." He turned back to the road, happy they both shut the hell up. "Now, you both are going to do exactly what I say. Absolutely no excuses." He pointed into the dark beyond the windshield. "You said they have a decent sized property? Dad, I'm going to drop you off in the woods behind the house, that way you can find a clear path through the woods and back to the road and the truck. After that, make your way through the woods and stay in the back yard. Keep an eye on the place. If any lights come on, I want you to text me immediately. Got it?"

"What are you going to do?" Fred asked.

"Ma and I are going inside. She's going to take the front, I'll take the back. We'll spread out and sweep the building."

Kay whined, "I don't *want* to go inside!"

"Too fucking bad. Would you rather stand out in the dark woods by yourself?"

She shook her head.

"Good, I didn't think so. Now shut up. Dad, you good with that?"

His father glanced out into the woods as they drove through the night. "Anything for Annie."

Edgar nodded. "That's what I like to hear."

When the orphanage bloomed in the darkness ahead, Edgar immediately clicked his headlights off and drove slowly past the front of the building, wanting to get a good, long look at the layout of the surroundings. No gate or fence around the front. No security officers. No lights burning on the inside. This had the potential to be a cake walk, if done right. He turned the truck onto the next road, which led around the dense forest to the back of the house. Once he found a spot to park along the road, all three jumped from the truck. Edgar took two small crowbars from behind the seat.

Edgar pointed at his father. "You know what to do." It wasn't a question.

"Can I at least get a flashlight?" Fred asked.

"No. No lights. This is supposed to be stealthy." He saw his father about to object, so he cut him short. "Don't ask again, pop."

Fred could only sigh as he headed into the woods.

"Ma, let's go."

She moaned, "Oh my lord, what are we doing?"

Edgar rolled his eyes. *If she doesn't shut the fuck up, I swear to God…*

They walked for maybe a half a mile, and each step brought another blustery complaint. "Let's go home, Eddy! Please! Let's go figure this out and do it the right way. I don't want to go to jail! I don't want *you* going to jail again! Annie needs her father to be clean and sober and—"

Before she could react, Edgar spun around and slapped his mother across the face. The crack of skin against skin echoed like a snapping branch. She stumbled and nearly lost her balance. As she started to speak, he stopped her dead. "If you speak another word, ma, I'm going to have to hurt you." He stepped closer with a jutting finger. "If you even so much as fucking fart, I'll break your goddamn neck and leave you in the ditch. You hear me, you loudmouth bitch? From here on out, *I* make the rules—and rule number one is zip it or be zipped. *Got it?*"

Holding her cheek, she nodded rapidly.

He lifted his finger up to his lips, then spun back around and headed toward the house.

A few minutes later, they were creeping across the meager parking lot in front of the orphanage. Edgar glanced up at the building. It was a bit larger up close than it looked from the road, but it wasn't too big. Three stories, multiple windows and doors, and, as far as his trained eyes could tell, absolutely no cameras or alarm systems. Unless his mother somehow ruined it, this heist would be fairly easy. He reached into his waistband and felt the stowed-away pistol.

He didn't plan to use it…but, hey, never say never.

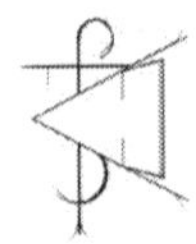

Fred cursed under his breath as he carefully walked through the dark. He was furious with how Edgar had spoken to them. He didn't care if his son was upset or stressed out, he was still their child. Back in his day, no one spoke to their elders with such vitriol. If everything went off without a hitch, he would have to teach that little shit some respect.

But there was a task at hand, and he intended on seeing it through…even if he couldn't exactly *see*. Beams of moonlight barely cut through the treetops, but it gave him just enough light to not fall on his face or rear end. Best not to hurt himself. He only had one job: find a clear path for them through the woods back to the truck. Easy peasy lemon squeezey.

Yet, it wasn't that easy. It felt as though he'd been walking for nearly twenty minutes and yet to locate the back of the house. It couldn't have been that far off the road...

Fred marched for another ten minutes or so, his frustration ballooning. At that point, he couldn't see a goddamn thing. He had promised his son no lights, nothing to give them away, but enough was enough. He took out his cell phone and activated the flashlight. Pointing it straight ahead, he nearly screamed.

Ten feet ahead was a little girl.

Her back was toward him. Her long blonde hair spilled over her shoulders in a tangled, ratty mess. Her pink, polka dot nightgown was smeared in several layers of dirt and grime.

From the back, she looked like Annie.

Fred took a moment to regain his composure, then took a few tentative steps toward the child. "Annie?" he whispered. "Annie, is that you, pumpkin?"

A few steps closer.

"Annie? What are you doing out here all by your lonesome, girl? It's not safe."

A little closer.

"Pumpkin, your daddy and your grandma are up at the house, looking for you. We've all come to take you home." He lightly placed his right hand on her shoulder. "How's about coming back to live with us at your real home?"

The girl he thought was Annie turned her head. Before he could pull his hand away, her mouth was on him. Teeth against flesh, she encased his thumb in her mouth and bit hard. Fred howled in pain. He tried to wrench his hand away, but the harder he pulled, the harder she clamped down. Her front teeth sank deeper, past the skin and tissue, now grating against the bone. When it seemed he would never get his hand back, he gave one last desperate yank, and his hand broke free from her lips.

His thumb didn't come back with it.

Screaming, he stumbled backward, his phone dropping from his grip, killing the light, and held his thumb-less hand against his chest. Blood sprayed across his shirt and neck, with thick gouts falling to the forest floor. The pain was like nothing he'd ever felt before. He stumbled backwards and could almost feel the warmth flee his body in an ice-cold cascade.

The little girl—who was definitely not Annie—sluggishly turned to face him. He gawked in horror.

Both of her eyes were gone.

Blood and bile obscured her features, both dripping down her face and chin in a viscous sludge. She chewed on the digit in her mouth, wheezing laboriously as the contents turned into a pink mush.

Feeling weak, Fred whimpered and turned to run back to the truck—

—only to find more children behind him.

Like the little girl, they were all covered head to toe in ruddy dirt. Their faces were a mess of dripping goop, and their eyes—*Their eyes! Where are their goddamn eyes?!*—were as gone as the moonlight above. Fred spun in each direction. They were everywhere, boxing him in. Nearly a dozen of them virtually appearing from thin air, their throats emitted thick, wet gurgles that filled his ears with pure hell. Blood wept from their empty eye sockets. They shambled closer. And closer.

Unsure what to do, Fred hollered and swung his free arm and struck a few, taking them down. But it wasn't enough. In a heartbeat, they were on him. Tiny hands pulled at his clothes. Adolescent teeth rent flesh from bone. Blood gushed from every hole, adding more color to the children's spoiled faces. Fred screamed and collapsed in a heap. The others feasted on his flesh, the little girl dropped down next to him. Grabbing his head, she pressed her cold face against his neck.

Despite the dozens of mouths mutilating his body, it was the one which ripped out his throat that hurt the very worst.

When her son disappeared around the side of the house, leaving her near the front door with a crowbar in her hand, Kay truly began to panic. Sure, she wanted Annie back in their lives in the worst way, but not like this. She'd done plenty of illegal things in her sixty-two years on planet earth, things that kept her up many nights, but none more regretful than this. Plenty of times she'd helped keep her son out of prison. She herself never considered it a future home. Maybe Edgar *did* have a plan, but at the moment, in the heat of the action, it sure felt like the biggest mistake any of them had ever made.

She glanced back at the street. Maybe she could make a run for it.

No…no, she couldn't leave Annie like that. Not her precious angel granddaughter. She put her metaphorical big girl pants on and made her way up to the front porch.

Ignoring the rhythmic throb in her cheek, she glanced from side to side, making sure she was alone. All was quiet. She stared nervously at the front door. Surely it would be locked and dead bolted. No way in hell they left this place unlocked with so many innocent souls sleeping inside. Despite the piece of curved steel in her grip, she reached for the door. Unexpectedly, the knob twisted easily in her grip, and the door swept open without a sound. Her heart began to pound.

She took a deep breath and stepped inside.

Unlike the chaotic scene the day before, the living room was now void of screaming, playing children. The pure silence was unnerving. She carefully moved into the foyer, mindful of the floor beneath her feet. So far it was free from creaking. She took a few more tentative steps, then closed the front door behind her.

This is wrong. This is so, so wrong.

"Eddy?" she whispered. *"Eddy?"* It appeared he wasn't inside yet, which meant she was all alone. Heart galloping, she turned back to the front door, ready to leave.

The ceiling creaked.

She immediately looked up. At first, she wasn't sure she'd actually heard it, but it repeated, this time slower and more drawn out, like someone was leaning forward on their toes. Her jaw shook, and her hands went numb.

"Eddy?" Silence. *"Fred?"*

She thought once more about fleeing, but she

couldn't disappoint Edgar again, or Annie for that matter. She took a deep breath and clenched her fists.

For Annie.

Her fear settled—at least, for the time being—she tiptoed through the living room and found the carpeted staircase on the far left end of the room. She prayed the steps would not creak under her weight, and thankfully, they did not speak her intrusion. She took them slow regardless.

Kay had no idea what floor Annie's room was on, but seeing as how there were both boys and girls staying under the same roof, she imagined they were being kept on different floors. She decided to try the second floor first. One look inside the first room, and she would be able to confirm her suspicions. But she had to be careful. There were three adults on hand at all times, and if she picked the wrong one, they may be in trouble a lot quicker than they had anticipated. She was suddenly thankful she was carrying the crowbar.

At the top of the first flight, she stepped out onto the landing. The narrow hallway beyond was lit only by a single blue light bulb, but that was enough to light her way. Each side of the corridor was lined with doors. Save for room numbers, the doors were bare and without character. It reminded Kay of a hospital, cold and lifeless. The sooner she could get her grandchild from this hellhole, the sooner she could get some color and fun back into her life.

She reached for the first knob and twisted.

Locked.

As were the next and the next.

Something wasn't right about this. Why would their rooms be locked at night? That seemed like an extreme safety hazard, something she would have to keep in mind depending on how this rescue mission went.

Somewhere up ahead, a floorboard creaked.

Kay spun toward it. "*Edgar*?" she whispered. "*Is that you?*" Despite her brain telling her not to, she crept on down the hall, gripping the crowbar tight. "*Edgar, answer me.*"

When she reached the sharp turn, she followed the path—then froze.

At the far end of the hallway, where a small window looked over the side yard, a man stood against the wall. Heart fluttering, it startled her, and for a moment she thought it was Edgar. It only took a few seconds to see it was not her son. The man was much taller and skinnier than Edgar, with far more hair, not at all the short, stalky grunt of a man he really was. The man's head was looking down, his chin touching his red Phillies T-shirt, as something dribbled from his mouth and pattered the carpet.

Kay wasn't sure what to do. He didn't appear to be one of the regular caretakers at St. Luke's, at least none that she recalled, and that terrified her fiercely. "I'm sorry!" she blurted, not knowing what to say.

The man slowly lifted his head.

Kay gasped.

Bright, fresh blood stained the man's ruined mouth. Between his shredded lips, a noxious black bile ran between the weathered yellow tombstones of his teeth, dripping down his chest and adding to the mess at his feet. His dead, clouded eyes glared her way as a bubbling moan gurgled from his throat. Kay mewled in fear as the liquid outpour increased from his maw, and with it came a wave of wriggling insects that tumbled onto the floor. The man then pitched forward, regurgitating loudly, and spat out a large wad of gray meat that went *splat* onto the pile.

Beetles and centipedes immediately dined on the remains of a severed tongue.

Screaming, Kay began to back up, her arms out in front of her. Her legs struck something low and solid behind her. Before she could catch herself from falling, her feet were already over her head. She shrieked. The crowbar flew from her grip, hitting the wall and bouncing away. A moment later, her head struck the floor with a sickening *thump*. Stars burst in her vision, momentarily blinding her. Dazed and unable to move, she blinked rapidly until her vision cleared up. Trembling, she dropped her head to side to see what she had tripped over.

It was a sheep.

Kay stared at the animal, utterly confused.

Unphased by her falling over it, the wooly creature spun around to face her, gazing down with black rectangular eyes.

How in the hell…

The creature bleated loudly, breaking the silence.

From around the hallway corner, something short trotted up beside it. Kay blinked again, unsure what she was seeing.

A pig had now joined them.

What in God's name—

Confusion morphed to terror as the large hog darted forward and clamped its jutting incisors directly into her cheek. Kay cried out in agony as the beast squealed and wrenched its blubbery pink head from side to side. Her soft facial skin tore in a long, wide strip, exposing her teeth beneath. Adding to her pain, the sheep followed suit and latched its mouth onto the fabric shielding her breast, grinding its teeth together around her nipple. When the pig finally ripped away her skin, blood sprayed across her face in warm, thick, crimson spurts. The sheep chewed away at her chest and sunk its long, stained face into the wound, gorging deeper into the fatty meat until it reached her chest plate. Kay tried to swat at the pig, catching it in the face, but the animal was faster. Much like it had her cheek, the pig latched onto her hand and snapped into her palm, biting down hard until both sets of teeth met in the middle. Blood sprayed in the fine mist, peppering its swollen pink face like freckles. Unable to move, Kay looked up as another large pig appeared over her face. Squealing loudly, its foul mouth encased her own, silencing her final scream before it could form.

The man at the end of the hallway watched on as he continued to vomit his filth.

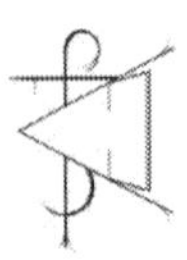

After not finding any unlocked windows on the side of the house, Edgar moved toward the rear. He hopped over the low fence and stood in the backyard. Other than the wind, which had suddenly picked up, all was quiet. That was good. That meant Mom hadn't caused any more commotion, and Dad was right where he was supposed to be. So long as they didn't fuck this up, this should go nice and smooth. If not—he pulled the pistol from his waistband and cocked the hammer—there was always ole Warbeck here to bark out a command or two. Keeping low, he crept along the length the house.

When he approached the porch, he found the back door sitting open.

He didn't even think to question it. He afforded a quick glance toward the livestock pens—*Animal pens? What the hell?*—then opened the screen door and stepped inside.

The kitchen was large and spacious. The scent of spices and cooked food immediately filled his nose. The sink to his left was overflowing with used pots and pans, and the stove was caked in grease and ancient stains. A small wooden plaque on the wall read **Jesus is the Answer**. Everything seemed old-fashioned and far past its natural expiration date. He wondered just how much money the state was funding this place to operate, if they were getting any money at all. If this was how the kitchen looked, he hated to know how the rest of this dump held up. Sitting the crowbar on the counter top, he held the pistol out before him and stalked toward the kitchen door, which he assumed led to the front of the house.

The basement door to his right slowly creaked open.

Edgar stopped and followed his gun toward the

noise.

The door continued to groan as it swung in his direction. When the opening reached a foot wide, it stopped. Edgar waited several seconds for someone to step out from behind, but no one did. He ground his teeth, now wondering if it was his mother, fucking with him. If it was, God help her ass…

He walked toward the door and peered around the opening. He squinted. At the bottom of the staircase, he saw the faint glow of candlelight. He turned back and glanced toward the kitchen door, wondering if he should keep on with the mission or if he should explore the building's depths. Someone was *definitely* down there, and the more he thought about it, the more his curiosity was piqued. Maybe Annie was down there, or maybe not, but either way he had the gun, and the gun made the rules wherever it went. He pulled the basement door open the rest of the way and carefully stepped down.

As he descended, he felt for a light switch but couldn't locate one. It didn't matter too much. The further down he went, the closer he got to the firelight. When he reached the bottom, his feet hit a dirt floor, which he found odd. For whatever reason he expected a finished basement, stocked with old boxes and lined with various canned foods or household supplies. What he found instead was a cavernous, hollow space, littered with large piles of dirt, some of which were waist high. A fire burning lamp was sitting at his feet, and beside it was an open book. Beyond the circle of light, the black swallowed everything whole.

Someone grunted in the dark.

Edgar narrowed his eyes. He took a step forward, trying to make out what he was seeing.

Several feet ahead of him, a young boy was furiously digging into the dirt. He held a small shovel, which he used to dig into the earth and then toss over his shoulder into a fresh pile beside him. He was down in a sizeable hole, maybe three or four feet in the ground. Filth and sweat was caked on his clothes. He had been here for some time.

The boy stopped and turned to Edgar. He was crying. "Help me, Mister."

Before Edgar could react, someone stepped up behind him. A second later, something long and very sharp split his skin and drove deep into his side. Eyes shooting wide, Edgar gasped in pain. The pistol flew from his grasp and landed in the dark. Before he could drop to his knees, a brown robed arm wrapped around his neck and held him up. Edgar gagged as it enclosed his throat.

Seeing this, the boy shrieked and went back to digging.

"Interloper..." a harsh voice whispered into his

ear. *"How dare you interrupt my progress?"*

Edgar grunted, "You m-mother...fucker..." Blood soaked his shirt and ran down his leg. "Wh-who are you?"

"Who am I?" they rasped, amused. *"I am the one who seeks the passage."*

"The wh-what?"

"The last artery between the worlds."

Through the pain, he watched as the child digging the hole dramatically slowed his pace. "I don't...*ah, fuck*...I don't understand."

The whispery voice chuckled. *"Of course you wouldn't. No one does... But I do."*

Finding himself growing weak, his blurry eyes dropped to the floor. They settled on the open book next to the lamp. Words and text he couldn't quite make out littered the pages, but that wasn't what grasped his attention. Crudely drawn faces of creatures and beings he couldn't quite comprehend had been inked into the center of each page. Things with too many eyes...and too many teeth...

The little boy suddenly collapsed and stopped moving.

The person holding him in place twisted the blade. Edgar howled in agony. He wanted to fight back, but he'd never been in so much pain in his life. He'd been beaten, burned, and had even overdosed, but this torture was so much worse. He wished he hadn't dropped his gun.

"Curses," they rasped, *"Donald was not the one. No matter. There are still more to continue the work. I will find the chosen one soon enough."*

The knife was ceremoniously extracted from his side, and a moment later Edgar was shoved forward toward the hole. He collapsed in a heap onto the hard dirt floor and gasped for air. The pain was tremendous, exquisite, and for a moment he wondered if this was the type of agony he had caused countless others over the course of his wasted life. He was quite sure of it.

The room filled with moans.

From out of the dark, dozens of eyeless, blood-covered children stumbled toward him. The little boy in the hole wheezed as he sat up and crawled toward him.

Edgar Willem Lashley soon found the pain in his side was only the appetizer before the main course.

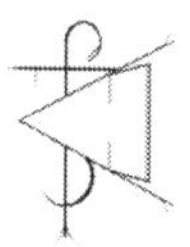

Dawn crested with gray dreary skies, and with that gloom came the realization that Brandon still hadn't come home. At some point, Jillian had moved to the couch to wait up for him, but she eventually fell asleep, and now her lower back was stiff. Groggy, she sat up and glanced around. She fumbled for her phone and checked for any responses. Nothing. Almost ten messages. Three calls. Zero response.

Instinctively, she wanted to be pissed off.

He'd promised her many times since they'd gotten the news of Bryce's adoption that he wouldn't do anything reckless. She'd allowed him that one drink, to numb the initial pain. Then, they would set about finding a solution. That was just her way. No sense in moping over shit. That took too much energy, which could be better spent finding a way *out* of the shit. If it was something out of her control, then it was best to move on. Brandon, on the other hand, was far more emotional. He tended to either stew over said shit or take careless actions, which usually did more harm than good.

She hoped like hell he hadn't done anything stupid last night.

After making a pot of strong coffee, she sipped it black and mulled over her next course of action. At one point, she considered calling Dan, but she quickly nixed that idea. He'd proven more than unhelpful, at best. A real creep, at worst. He hadn't changed one bit. She shouldn't have expected he ever would have.

Smoke, her wolfdog, came up and licked her hand. Smiling, Jillian got up and dumped some kibble into his bowl. He greedily scarfed it down.

By the time she settled back on the couch, she'd decided to drive out to Chadds Ford herself. She'd go to the police and tell them the truth; that she believed her boyfriend had come into town that night and what he was looking for. It just felt right. She'd known Brandon long enough to understand how he worked. It would be just like him to try heading out there himself, doing something dumb and selfish. Hell, for all she knew he was already in jail. Either way, she intended to mention Saint Luke's. There was something odd going on there. So much secrecy. Plus, Dan hadn't seemed right at all since leaving there. For all his faults, he wasn't the type to scare easily, and that rattled her.

Before getting up to leave, she hooked a leash onto Smoke's collar.

"Come on, boy. We're going for a ride."

Though the sun ultimately emerged from the early morning grayness, the scenic drive to Chadds

Ford had lost all its luster. Jillian's focus remained on the road ahead as she played over in her mind what she'd say to the police. She ran the script beginning to end, took great pains to slow the thoughts that wanted so badly to race. In the back of the car, Smoke panted happily, not a care in the world. She was jealous.

Chadds Ford was one of those last vestiges of small-town America. Mostly houses tucked away on swaths of shaded woodlands. The rest of town was centered around Main Street, complete with Mom-and-Pop shops and enough benches for the town elderly to sit upon and sneer at outsiders. They even had a General Store, Woodhouse's Goods 'N Such, complete with wood paneling and a large barrel to drop cigarette butts in. She couldn't remember the last time she'd seen one of those. At the end of the street was a small police station. It was a near-perfect cube, built from sepia-toned brick, with very few windows, and a glass door with POLICE stenciled in now peeling letters.

Jillian kept the windows cracked, cut the engine and got out.

"Be right back, boy," she said to the dog.

She collected herself, fighting the urge to yank open the station door, instead opening it gently. The reception area was empty and quiet. It smelled dusty and dry. There was a desk behind Plexiglas, but no one was sitting in it.

"Hello?" she called. No one answered. She hardened her voice. "Hello?"

Her gaze flitted to a bulletin board. A handful of missing kid posters, all recent, stood out to her. There was also a bizarre PSA about warning signs that someone you know might be into Satan. The poster boasted highly dated stereotypes about wearing all black, veganism, and listening to heavy metal or Soundcloud rap. It was an odd thing to see in a police station. Law enforcement was supposed to be a secular institution. Then again, this was the sticks.

"Help you?" someone behind her asked.

She turned to face a broad-shouldered cop with white hair and a trim mustache. He stood behind the bulletproof partition, arms folded and wearing a severe expression. She thought he looked a little too old to still be wearing a badge, but maybe he was just a desk jockey? She put on her best smile.

"Hi! I'm hoping you can help me."

He smiled without showing teeth. "I can try."

"I'm looking for someone I think may have passed through here. My boyfriend."

The cop cocked an eyebrow. "Lucky guy."

Warmth bloomed in her cheeks. "Thanks. Anyway, he was looking for his little brother who was...well, he was at St. Luke's but got adopted."

The cop's eyebrow raised even higher. Jillian immediately felt stupid. She had this all planned out, but now hearing it out loud, with her heart pounding a mile a minute, made her feel like this was all a mistake. They wouldn't see things her way. How could she expect them to? As far as they—and she—knew, St. Luke's hadn't done a damn thing wrong. Sure, the place seemed weird, but she had no real proof of wrong doing. *Don't bring up St. Luke's. Talk about Brandon. You're looking for Brandon.*

"He's been under a lot of pressure lately," she quickly added. "My boyfriend."

"Is he dangerous?"

"What? No."

"Not even to himself?"

"I don't … think so."

"You don't *think so*?"

She sighed to avoid speaking with too much emotion. "Look, can't I just file a missing person report or something?"

He flashed her a smile that she hated. "Sure thing. It's a free country, right?" He buzzed her in the side door and held out an inviting hand. "Have a seat."

What followed was a series of generic questions about Brandon's appearance. Whether or not he used drugs or carried weapons. The last time she saw him.

Any idea where he might have gone. He typed her answers into a computer, hunting and pecking the letters on a bulky, outdated keyboard.

"You said something about St. Luke's?"

Jillian hesitated. "Yeah, why?"

He shook his head. "No reason."

"Are you sure?"

"You think he may have been headed that way?"

"I mean, I don't know. Just a, well, a hunch, I guess."

"Watch a lot of cop shows?"

"Not really."

He clicked something, looked over the screen and pressed his lips together. Then, he pushed away from the desk.

"Okay," he said. "He's in the system."

"In the system?"

"Yep. We'll be on the lookout."

"So, that's it?"

He shrugged one shoulder. "Be sure to reach out if you think of anything else that might help."

"Yeah," she mumbled. "Yeah, thanks."

"Ma'am," the officer said and dipped his head in a nod.

Jillian left the station feeling very cold.

When she reached her car, a shadow dropped over her. Inside the car, her dog went nuts, barking and snarling with defensive agitation. Jillian spun and stepped back, sucking in a seething breath.

A short, mostly bald man with wisps of hair combed over his dome stood near her car. He wore an old-fashioned tweed sports coat and faded blue jeans. Thick glasses made his eyes appear larger than they probably were. Under the sports coat, he wore a black T-shirt with *Necrophagia* printed across the chest in red, drippy font. He looked way too old to be wearing a band T-shirt, but she supposed stranger things had happened. His bearded face scowled.

"What the hell, man?" she said, her tone a harsh whisper.

She didn't want to yell and draw the attention of the police. Even if this guy had evil intentions, his age likely gave him some physical limitations. She suspected a kick to the shin or the balls would drop him pretty quickly. Or she could just open the door and let Smoke rip out his throat.

"What do you know about Hell, *signorina*?" The man spoke with a thick accent. She thought it might be Italian. "Do you know about the seven doorways of evil?"

Jillian pulled a face. "Yeah, whatever, old man. I'll just be on my way." She made to head for her car door. The man didn't move out of her path. She stopped and put her hands on her hips. Smoke had stopped barking, but was still growling, low and menacing. "You gonna let me pass or what?"

"There is one right here. In Chadds Ford. At the orphanage."

She lowered her hands and her guard. "Excuse me? Why would you say that?"

"Because I know why you're here."

Despite her cynicism, she felt a spark of hope. "Wait—have you seen Brandon?"

"No. But I have a seen many other things. I've looked inside the fire and yet my eyes remain."

With a groan, she pushed past him. "All right, old man. You want to talk about demons and shit, you've got the wrong gal." She got her car door open. The old man stood aside and stuffed his hands in his pocket. His eyes still looked cartoonishly large as he watched her movements. "Now, if you'd excuse me." She slid into the driver's seat and reached for the push ignition.

"He came looking for his brother, did he not?" the old man asked.

Her hand froze an inch from the button. "What did you say?"

"Brandon. Your friend. He came looking for one of the children."

She glanced down the street, not sure what to think now. This guy was clearly not all there, perhaps a few bowling pins short of a strike, but he was onto something. She didn't know anything about evil doorways or Hell, but Brandon was missing. He had disappeared for the very same reason the old man stated. Further down the street, she spotted a tavern called MacColl's.

She turned back to the strange fellow, feeling a bit less tense. "Buy you a drink, old man?"

He fidgeted, looking past her. "That would be lovely."

"All right. Well, get in."

He got into the passenger seat, and she started the engine. The man in her car smelled like old books and ash. She worried how her dog would react, but thankfully Smoke had gone completely docile. He leaned between the front seats to lick the back of the old man's head. Jillian gave her passenger a small smile and put the car in gear.

"So, what's your name?" she asked, reversing out of the parking spot.

"Claudio."

"I'm Jill."

She inched her vehicle forward, examining the quaintness of the town in her periphery. It looked so innocent. Not the sort of place you'd go looking for missing loved ones…which, of course, made it exactly the right place for that very thing. You didn't have to be a horror movie aficionado to know that. It was always the quaint, nonthreatening places that housed the worst depravity behind its closed doors, shallow graves in the surrounding woods.

She parked in front of MacColl's and stopped the car. Smoke emitted a whine.

"So, what's good here?" she asked.

"I'm not a local, so I don't know. I only drink Chianti."

She laughed. "Fancy."

They got out of the car, and Jillian brought Smoke with them. She led him on his leash to a bench, tied him to it, and entered the tavern with Claudio. The place was teeming with cigarette smoke. An AC/DC song blared on the sound system. Biker types and hipsters stood around pool tables, while some sat by their lonesome at the bar. A few of them turned to look at the new entrants, but most kept to what they were doing. She ordered Claudio his wine, which she was surprised they even had, and got herself a lager. She wasn't a big drinker, but she didn't have a problem like Brandon either. It didn't bring out anything in her; it just helped her relax. They found a table away from any loudspeakers, but she still had to shout to be heard as AC/DC gave way to a KISS anthem.

"So, how did you know why my boyfriend came up here?" she asked.

Claudio took a sip from his stemware, then rubbed his hands together. "I know many things. Lots of things people forget. But the forgotten things, they don't forget."

Jillian sighed. "Seriously, man? Riddles?"

"Not a riddle. These are facts. *Verità o silenzio.*"

"Do you know where Brandon is or not?"

"I only know what I know. There are places. This is one of those places."

Jillian was starting to regret taking this guy with her. Still, he had to know something. Maybe. She decided to try a different approach.

"Okay, fine. You want to talk? Let's talk. You mentioned Hell and doorways. Care to elaborate?"

"Will you believe me?"

"I'll listen."

He looked away, seeming to ponder this. Finally, he nodded. "There are seven doorways—gates, if you will. Seven gates to Hell. Seven evil spirits. Forty years ago, several were opened in other cursed places. North in Dunwich. South in New Orleans. An island in the Antilles. A small fishing village in Sicily. Much like this place I seek, I was summoned to stop all of these. But...but I was always one step behind. Always too late."

She felt a small chill move across her skin. A memory materialized from a fog of forgetfulness. One lonely night spent surfing the 'net as a teenager. She found this ridiculous blog by some guy who swore up and down that in the late seventies, zombies had overrun the streets of New York and a bunch of people were killed, including some police and the staff of a radio station. Of course, this never happened. It would've been much bigger news. But this guy was absolutely convinced, enough to dedicate tens of thousands of words to his rants and raves. He had all these weird grainy photos of supposed attacks during the incident. She thought of this now because she could have sworn that the blogger had said the outbreak had begun on one of the Antilles islands. What fascinated her most about those blogs was the writer didn't compose like a crazy person. He wrote very cogently, and he never asked for money or anything. There was no apparent agenda beyond making sure people knew about the New York City zombie outbreak of '79.

Much like that blogger, this elderly foreigner,

Claudio, didn't sound terribly unhinged either. A little scattered, yeah, but he spoke deliberately and clearly, especially now that he had a willing audience. He didn't sound crazy, nor was he asking for anything, at least not yet. Maybe that was shaky logic for determining the truth of someone's statements, but it made sense to her, especially now when she was worried so much about her closest companion.

"So, what's this have to do with St. Luke's?" She thought about the poster in the police station. "Are they devil worshippers or something? Small town Satanists?"

His features hardened. His eyes blinked. "*Signorina*, it's not as simple as gods and devils. These are simplistic notions, dreamed up to make sense of what is beyond comprehension."

"But you said these were gates to Hell, right?"

"*Hell* is just the word we give it."

"And there's one of those gates where? At the orphanage?"

"*Sì.*"

"And someone there wants to open it?"

"Unfortunately."

A sinking feeling washed over her. She didn't believe in the supernatural or gates to the underworld, but she *did* believe that people were capable of terrible things when they had radical beliefs. Atrocities like

9/11 and the bombings of abortion clinics immediately came to mind. What if they were doing something awful to these children? What if they'd done something terrible to Brandon?

"We need some kind of proof," she said. He watched her without making an expression. "Then, maybe we can go to the police with evidence."

"They will be of no help," he declared. "We need to seal the gate ourselves." Claudio reached into his sports coat and extracted a brass object that looked like something between a religious object and a large key. A dark, ruby substance shifted inside of it.

Jillian eyed him suspiciously. "I don't know, man."

"Please! Those fools at St. Luke's will not listen to me. But you? You are nonthreatening. Have a nice face. Pretty American girl. Perhaps they will be more forthcoming. Give you some information."

"Like what?"

"Some clue to the gate's location. Then, maybe we go after dark to seal it."

She pointed at the table. "What's that key? It looks like there's something in it."

"It contains the blood of saints," he said, proudly. "Plus, liquefied silver."

"Shit, really? How's it stay liquid?"

"Not everything is explainable. *Accettiamo il*

misterioso, anche se non ci accetta."

"And that means?"

"We accept the mysterious, even if it does not accept us."

She pounded the rest of her beer and folded her hands. "All right, look. I don't know how much of this I believe. If I'm *really* honest, it's probably very little."

Claudio shouted, "It does not matter what you believe! It cares not if you do not accept voodoo curses or Egyptian talismans! Or warlocks or immoral clergyman! I have seen it all with my own eyes, *signorina,* every terrible occurrence, and I can tell you they do not care one bit. They are as real as you and I, and if we do nothing but flap our gums like children, I can promise you are going to see the worst of it all...how you say...up close and personal."

Jillian noticed nearly everyone in the bar had turned to stare at them both. Her face flushing red, she held out her hands. "Hey, calm down. Look, I didn't mean to insult you. It's just a lot to take in all at once. Okay? But I'll tell you this: any chance I can uncover anything about what happened to Brandon or his little brother is worth taking. As weird as you are, I guess I'm glad I ran into you."

"It is not so random," he said, pointing a boney, arthritic finger. "I had a feeling—a *premonizione*—I needed to be outside that very police station around the time you came out."

She humored him with a smirk but didn't believe his fatalism for a second. "Can we head up there now?"

He clutched the brass key to his chest and pocketed it again.

"I think the sooner the better. We're running out of time."

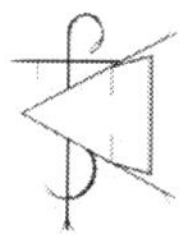

It was the only good restaurant in town, Salvati's Deli, and Kurt intended to enjoy his club sandwich, macaroni and cheese, and Diet Dr. Pepper in peace while he finished his mountain of paperwork. He normally ate his lunches at St. Luke's, but Myra and Lionel had been using the living room near his office for game time with the children. Kurt cared for the kids, but there was only so much screaming and raucous laughter a man could take. He let the other two know he'd be back later that evening. Now that he was alone, he could finally get some work done.

His solitude didn't last long.

As he thumbed through the paperwork, mayonnaise dotting his wiry beard, he was suddenly aware of the two shadows that now stood over his table. He crossed a t and dotted an i, and without looking up he asked, "Can I help you?"

"Where are the children?"

Kurt scrunched his face. "Excuse me?"

"You heard me, *signore*. The children. Where are they?"

He finally glanced up to the odd pair before him. The one who had spoken to him with growling disdain was an old man, somewhere on the wrong side of eighty, with combed-over white hair, and a sneer that suggested he hadn't smiled in half a lifetime. His thick Italian accent was way out of place for this backwoods town, but so was the young woman next to him. Not sharing his stern glare, she appeared hesitant and apologetic, even nervous. Kurt sighed, expecting yet another rant from angry relatives of one of his charges.

Pinching the bridge of his nose, he sighed. "If you're here to rant about your adopted child or grandchild, I can assure you you're wasting your breath. Take it to a state judge."

The old man narrowed his eyes. "That is not what I speak of, and you know it."

"No, mister, I don't know what you're speaking of."

"I speak of Hell!" Hands balled, the old man

smacked his fist on the table, nearly knocking over Kurt's soda.

"Hey, damn it!"

"I speak of awakened evil! And of innocent lives lost! *Scemo! Ti maledico!*"

The woman quickly stopped the old man from hitting the table again. "Hey, hey, hey, I think we're getting a little heated, Claudio. Cool your jets."

"I know not what that means," he growled.

"It means settle down. You're causing a scene." She turned to Kurt with an embarrassed smile. "My apologies, Mr…"

Kurt wiped his hands on a napkin. "Wiser. Kurt Wiser."

"Mr. Wiser, I'm so sorry for intruding on your meal like this. My friend here spotted you from across the street and nearly leapt from my moving car to come in here."

"Does your friend have a name, or do I call him 'Where Are They?'"

"Sorry, this is Claudio, and my name is Jillian."

"Charmed."

She nodded uncomfortably. "Yes, well, again, we didn't mean to cause a scene like this, but I believe Claudio here and myself have a few questions to ask you. You work at St. Luke's, right?"

Kurt eyed his sandwich and sighed. "If you

must know, yes, I am the overseeing manager of St. Luke's. And as you can see, I have a literal mountain of paperwork to complete, as well as a lunch to finish, so if you could please get to the point, it would be much appreciated."

The old Italian man, Claudio, shifted his feet as though he were going to speak, but Jillian spoke up instead. "I realize this is awkward, but my boyfriend, Brandon, went missing recently. I think he went looking for his little brother…at St. Luke's."

Kurt crossed his arms. "When was this?"

"Just a few days ago."

"That would definitely explain the broken window in my office," he grumbled.

Her eyes went wide. "So he *was* there?"

"If the minus four hundred dollars from the company bank account means anything, then it appears he was. And before you ask, no he's not there anymore, but if I see him myself, I'm contacting the authorities. You can be assured of that."

"That won't be necessary," Claudio said.

Frowning, Kurt turned back to him. "Who are you again?"

"Someone who sees through your lies."

"Excuse me?"

Claudio placed both hands on the table and leaned in. "You have no idea what you have caused on those grounds—what your continued presence stirs. Even without opening it, being near it influences anything with a beating heart. You, sir, have damned us all."

Now it was Kurt's turn to smack the table, fuming. "*That's enough!* I believe I've had my fill of the both of you, coming in here and speaking to me in this manner. You both need to leave before I call the police and they force you to leave."

Jillian appeared to panic. "Mr. Wiser, I'm so sorry! All we're looking for is answers."

"What do you want from me, lady? You have a problem with me? My orphanage? My workers or my kids? Take a number. It seems like everyone is upset with me these days."

Claudio sneered, eyeing them both. "There will be no number to take if we continue to delay."

His patience wearing dangerously thin, Kurt steeled himself, aware of the curious eyes of the other customers around them. "Listen, you two, I am a *very* busy man. My bullshit meter has now hit red. Please, for the love of God, leave me be."

"Mr. Wiser—Kurt—all I want to know is where Brandon went." Tears rimmed Jillian's eyes. "Or, at the very least, where his little brother, Bryce, is. If I can get some sort of location for him, then maybe I can locate my boyfriend."

Kurt shook his head. "Miss, you know very well I can't freely give out confidential information like that. You would have to go through the proper channels, and even then, it's not a guarantee."

"Please. At the very least can you give me confirmation Bryce was adopted out. Brandon seemed to think he wasn't."

"That's absurd. What else would have happened to him?" He reluctantly went through his paperwork and found the child's release papers. "Bryce Campbell? Right here."

"And what about Mary Funches?" asked Claudio. "Donald Baterman? Jake Brooks? Berrshod Jennings? Kilah Hill?"

Kurt eyed him with suspicion. "How do you know those names?"

"Where are those children?"

"Answer my question?"

"Answer *my* question, Mr. Wiser. Where are they?"

Kurt growled, "Legally, that's none of your damn business, but if you must know, they're all safe and healthy within the confines of St. Luke's."

Claudio feigned surprise. "*Are* they?"

"Absolutely."

He nodded to the paperwork on the table. "I'll bet those say differently."

"Excuse me?"

"Check your papers, *signore.*"

"Why? I know what I have—"

"Check it again," Claudio insisted. "How do you American's say…humor me."

Wanting nothing more than to shut this old man up, Kurt begrudgingly leafed through his files. He didn't need this shit. He didn't need a couple of complete strangers verbally roughing him up like this in public. Though he lived a bit closer to the city, he liked to think he was a stand-up member of this town. Someone respectable. Someone who offered a valuable service to the community at large. Someone who…

"Wait a second."

Confused, Kurt pulled out a form from his stack. He stared hard at the name across the top.

Donald Baterman

Below that: **APPROVED FOR EXPOUSAL**

"I never approved this." His eyes scanning the form, they drifted down until they found the release signature at the bottom of the page. "What?"

It was signed by Richard Martel. Dick.

"This…doesn't make sense."

Jillian leaned over the table to look. "What? What's wrong?"

"Well…two things. One, this child should still

be an active charge at St. Luke's. I've never once had any potential candidates court him. Not under my watch. And two, my boss, Dick Martel, the proprietor, doesn't sign the children out. I do. That's literally *my* job."

He speedily flipped through the rest of the stack and was shocked to find more release forms…each one with names they shouldn't boast. Brooks. Jennings. Hill. Young. Rice. Washington. Funches. And on and on. Even the names of the adoptive parents didn't ring a bell. Sure, he'd been busy lately, maybe not as mentally present as he should be, but he was a busy man, spending most of his days running errands and keeping the orphanage running like clockwork. All at the request of…

Kurt met Claudio's eyes. "How did you know?"

The old man stood up straight and glared down at the Kurt through his nose. "Evil is evergreen to those who are sworn to fight it. This is not my first rodeo, so to speak. This evil I seek has been building for some time. It calls to me because it's spreading. And the closer they get to the gate, the worse the evil will get. I have seen more than you could ever know, Mr. Wiser. Things that would make you want to pluck out your own eyes so you could never witness the horror. What you are sitting on is the final gate to Hell, and you're too stupid to even know it."

Shaking, Kurt stood to eye level with them both. "Listen, mister, I don't know who you are or what the hell you're talking about, but I do know this. Something is *very* off. Now, if you'll excuse me." He pulled out his wallet, slapped a twenty dollar bill on the table, snatched his jacket up, and quickly walked around them both.

Jillian asked, "Where are you going?"

"I need to speak to Mr. Martel. He has some explaining to do."

Claudio buttoned his coat. "Then we go with you, hmm?"

Kurt hesitated, taking a deep, uneasy breath, then nodded, urging them to follow.

The house was quiet. *Way* too quiet. While there were a few kids milling about the living room, either playing board games or putting together puzzles, Annie wasn't sure where everyone else was hiding. Maybe in their rooms, keeping to themselves? Perhaps some even went to bed early?

There was such a dour mood these days, Annie

wasn't even sure what day it was anymore. Not that it mattered. Tomorrow could have been Christmas day and it would have felt like any normal Tuesday. Days didn't matter much when you had no one to share them with. When the few people you cared about were now gone and everyone else was not their normal selves, it was hard to want to be around anybody, which was why she preferred to be alone.

As the sun went down, and the crisp fall air snacked on uncovered flesh, Annie stood outside by herself, staring into the animal pens. While the sheep in the adjacent pen were quiet, the two hogs in the enclosure next to them were causing an awful racket. Annie observed intently as they ran into one another, fighting for something loose in the middle of the mud. She carefully crawled up the wooden slats of the fence and leaned in, wanting to get a better look. The hogs snapped and snorted, tearing at the pale, mud-covered object.

Annie's eyes went wide. Her lips pulled back from her teeth.

They were fighting over a severed hand.

Horrified, she gawked at the loose human body part, wondering where it came from. The glint of a wedding ring was struck by the last of the sunlight, and it only took a matter of seconds before Annie recognized Grandma Kay's gaudy jewelry. The hogs took both ends of the hand and tore away at the whitish flesh, revealing greyed muscle and bone beneath. Dark blood oozed like oil from the wrist stump and smeared across the pig's snouts. Annie gagged and nearly threw up—

—but a hand fell onto her shoulder, making her shriek instead.

"Annie, hon," Miss Myra said, looking down, "what are you doing out here?"

Catching her breath, Annie quickly turned back to the pigs.

The pen was now empty. No sign of the two animals or the hand anywhere.

"But..." Annie started. She searched the dark enclosure, confused, not finding either creature.

"What's the matter?"

Annie shook her head, confused. "Nothing. It's...nothing."

"Okay, silly. Whatever you say. Come on." She guided Annie toward the back door. "It's getting a bit too cool out here. No need to catch a cold. I've got a fire going. Let's go warm up."

Shrugging her off, Annie took a few steps back. "Miss Myra?"

The adult turned back with a concerned look. "Yes?"

"Where is everyone?"

"What do you mean?"

"Where *is* everyone? Where did everyone go?"

Miss Myra pursed her lips. "Well, Mister Kurt stepped out for the night, Mister Lionel is cleaning the upstairs bathrooms, and many of the other children are playing in their rooms."

Annie made sure to keep her eyes on Miss Myra's. "No, I mean where are Edna and Donnie and everyone else?"

"Hon, Edna was adopted by a nice family from Lancaster, and Donnie…well, we felt it would be better if he resided somewhere else. He was transferred because he was the subject of bullying by a few of your peers."

Annie crossed her arms and frowned. "I don't believe you."

Looking shocked, Miss Myra asked, "Whatever do you mean?"

"Donnie was just here yesterday. I didn't see anyone come to get him."

"They came early like they always do."

"And Edna? I saw her toys in the burn barrel."

"What?"

"And I've seen her…" Annie's eyes drifted to the woods beyond the yard. "…out there."

Miss Myra's gaze followed hers, lingering on the darkness between the trees, then drifted back.

"Hon, you're completely mistaken. By law, we're forced to discard any belongings left behind by any children. It's a health concern to leave out any sort of odds and ends like that, so we trash it or, in this case, burn it to help kill the spread the potential germs. And as far as Donnie and Edna go, our adoptions and transfers happen early morning before anyone is awake, so not to disturb or upset the others. Mister Kurt, Mister Lionel, or Mister Martel take care of that, usually before even I wake up."

As much as Annie wanted to stand her ground, Miss Myra's explanation *did* make sense. She imagined she would probably be upset if she had to watch others being ceremoniously taken away by new parents, while others like her, who had been stuck at St. Luke's for some time, watched on. Still, something didn't feel right to her. The aura around the house was on a steady decline, and Annie seemed to fight against it every day to stay above the surface.

"Do you not feel safe?" Miss Myra asked.

Annie wanted to say no, but she simply shrugged instead.

Miss Myra approached and placed both hands on Annie's shoulders. "I know you're lonely, hon. I get it. More children will come. Until then, we can be the best of friends." She smiled sadly and gave Annie a gentle squeeze. "Such a strong kid. You've been through so much in your young life. More than anyone could ever know." She combed Annie's hair behind her ear and stared at her for a long while. "So strong."

There was another few moments of awkward staring before she added, "Come back inside. I have something I want to show you."

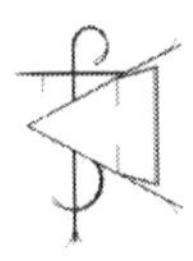

Not surprisingly, Jillian was having second thoughts. As they all drove to Mr. Martel's house, a person she didn't know from Adam, she chastised herself for not being smarter and just going home. All she wanted was to locate Brandon, or at the very least find his trail, and now she was somehow following a strange old man as he chased supernatural beings and attempted to locate a gate to Hell. *What in God's name am I doing?* She wished she had brought some form of protection, a gun or even pepper spray, but she supposed Smoke would have to do. The enormous dog sat between her and Claudio in the backseat, panting happily as Kurt steered the SUV.

The house they were searching for wasn't far, maybe ten miles outside of Chadds Ford, but it felt like an eternity. All three remained relatively silent for the ride. While she contemplated her choices, Claudio grumbled to himself, whispering what she assumed were Italian slurs. In the front seat, Kurt Wiser shook his head, fighting a war of internal words. Both men were severely on edge, which put Jillian, someone who normally preferred to keep a level head, on the nervous threshold. By the time they reached the house, all three couldn't wait to jump out of the car.

The home of Dick Martel was much larger than she expected. Two stories and a multi-car garage, there weren't homes like this in the south end of Philadelphia where she resided. Bright white latticing was positioned up the sides of the vinyl walls, with dark green vines weaving between the wooden slats. A well-manicured lawn, clean windows, a small garden sign boasting a state-of-the-art security system. Yes, this was far nicer than she was used to. But there was something off. Even though an expensive-looking BMW sedan was parked by its lonesome out front, every light in the house was off. She checked her phone, discovering it was only after 6 PM. Unless Mr. Martel was elderly, it would be strange for him to already be asleep.

The wind abruptly picked up and ruffed their clothes.

"Is he home?" Claudio asked, eyeing the house.

Kurt nodded. "Should be. That's his car. Not sure where else he could be. He doesn't do much these days. He's retired, mostly using St. Luke's as a tax write-off."

After making sure Kurt had a window cracked for Smoke, they marched up to the porch. Kurt rapped on the door three times and waited.

No answer.

His face pinched, Claudio looked past him. "When was the last time you saw Mr. Martel?"

"Let's see…" Kurt rubbed his beard. "Honestly? I can't remember. I normally just drop off the paperwork in his mailbox. He's a private man and doesn't like to be bothered."

"Spoken to him lately?"

"No. Lionel, one of my two live-in caretakers, spoke to him for me just the other day to discuss funds—" Kurt turned to Jillian. "—for a new window."

Jillian rolled her eyes.

When no one answered, Kurt knocked once more, this time a bit harder. "Mr. Martel? Dick? Are you home? It's Kurt Wiser from St. Luke's."

Tired of waiting, Claudio reached for the doorknob. A moment later he opened the door and stepped inside.

"Hey," Kurt called, "you can't do that!"

"And yet I did."

"Son of a—"

Jillian pushed past him. "Come on."

Behind her, Kurt huffed and joined them indoors.

The house was much warmer than Jillian expected. It was only early October and still a bit warmer in direct sun. There was no reason for anyone to have their heater on quite yet. Jillian took a look around. The furniture was outdated by at least a few decades, nearly everything made from stained, polished oak. In the front hallway, both walls were lined with an assembly of dusty photographs. Each one contained Mr. Martel himself, a squat, heavyset man with bright rosy cheeks and a smile that touched each ear. He was shaking hands with nearly everyone. Politicians, celebrities, musicians—he appeared to be a worldly man. If Jillian wasn't so scared, she would have been impressed.

Jillian asked, "What did he do for a living?"

Kurt stood beside her. "Mostly stocks and bonds, but he owned a lot of businesses up and down the east coast. Worked for the local government, too, I believe. I'm guessing that's how he became involved with the orphanage." He glanced up at the staircase. "Mr. Martel? Are you home? It's Kurt from St. Luke's. Don't be alarmed."

Jillian peeked into the living room. "I don't think he's here."

"Oh, he's here," Claudio mumbled.

"Maybe we spread out?" Kurt suggested. "Take it slow to not scare him if he's asleep. He's an old man."

While Claudio searched the kitchen, Jillian decided she wanted no part of spreading out. She stayed close to Kurt, who crept down the hallway toward the back of the house.

"Dick? You awake?" He stopped and cocked his head.

"What?" she asked.

"Do you hear that?"

At first, she heard nothing, save for her own heartbeat, but then she caught it. It was faint, but she could make out something. Something *wet*. A squishy noise, like someone squeezing wet pasta in a fist over and over. A tentative few steps further, and the squelching rose in volume. She couldn't put her finger on what it was, but deep in her guts she knew, unlike a refrigerator running or an air conditioner kicking on, it wasn't a normal household sound. Judging by Kurt's face, he was thinking the very same thing.

At the end of the hall, they found a set of closed double doors. Claudio quietly joined them. Kurt's outstretched hand froze in place.

"What the..." Jillian felt her stomach clench.

Both brass door handles were covered in large gray worms. They squirmed and crawled over one another, falling off and pattering the carpet like loose change. His face pinched with disgust, Kurt glanced over to Claudio, who eyed him back, as if expecting this. The elderly man brushed off the bugs with his bare hands, then slid open both doors.

Jillian screamed.

The floor was alive with worms. They wriggled and writhed like a living carpet, nearly half a foot deep, filling every square inch of walking space. They fell from the open doorway, spilling out onto their feet by the hundreds.

Sitting behind the desk near the rear of the room was Dick Martel.

Much like the floor beneath them, his rotting corpse was covered in a twisting, buzzing mass of grave flies and flesh-eating maggots. There was very little left of the stout man; he had been reduced to little more than an upright carcass. The warmth of the house, combined with the closed room, had trapped his putrefying odor, which now hit their noses like a sledgehammer to the face. Jillian turned back to the hallway and vomited.

"My God..." Kurt croaked.

Stone-faced, Claudio watched on. "Now do you

believe, *signore*?"

"I…don't know what to believe," he whispered. His face flushed stark white.

Jillian wiped her mouth with her sleeve. "We need to call the police!"

Claudio lifted his hand. "No. Not yet." To Kurt, "Would Mr. Martel have any paperwork on-hand for St. Luke's? A deed, perhaps?"

Kurt couldn't take his eyes off his decomposing boss. "I imagine so, yes."

"Then we search." Unbothered by the bugs, Claudio stepped into the room. *"L'inferno ci consumerà tutti. Dio ci aiuti."*

Taking a deep breath, Kurt joined him.

Jillian truly didn't want to follow, but she knew she had to help. Horrified, she took careful steps, her shoes sinking into the squirming worms. The further she advanced, the more they sank into her socks. "Oh God."

While Claudio pulled apart the bookcase, tossing books and papers aside onto the floor, Kurt searched through a filing cabinet near the window. That left Jillian with the desk. Near the dead body. She approached with caution. Though she didn't actually expect the man's fetid corpse to wake up and leap after her, the sight and smell of it was almost too much to bear. Eyes down and breathing from her mouth, she stepped around the desk and carefully opened the top drawer. Pens, paper, paperclips, and several rolls of lip balm rolled around loose inside. She closed it and went for the bottom drawer.

"Jesus..."

More worms crawled through the inside of the cabinet, their fat, ropey bodies lying on top of a large stack of files. Groaning in disgust, she reached in and shook off the bugs, extracting the top stack. The logo of a realty company was embroidered on the cover. "You guys, I think I found something."

Kurt stepped around Dick's body. "May I?" She handed him the file, which he opened and leafed through.

Claudio joined them. "What did you find? What is it?"

His eyes scanning the pages, Kurt shook his head, frowning. "This...doesn't make any sense. How can this be?"

"What? Speak up."

"There's no mention of Dick as the sole owner. In fact, according to these signatures he's only leasing it."

"Then who owns the building?" Jillian asked.

Kurt looked up from the file, his mouth pulled back in confusion and shock. "Myra Jones..."

Claudio grunted. "How fast can you drive?"

By the time they reached St. Luke's, the wind had whipped up into a tempestuous frenzy. The trees in the surrounding woods swayed and circled like worshippers in a pagan ritual. Food wrappers, paper bags, and dead leaves swirled and tossed about in the air. A camp chair tumbled end over end across the orphanage's yard. The wind howled in a dissonant scale. It sounded like a living thing, some great beast awakened after decades of hibernation, and none too pleased at its revival. In the backseat of Kurt's SUV, Smoke alternated between high whines and guttural growls.

"What's happening?" Jillian asked, no longer concerned with keeping cool or hiding panic from her voice.

"The gate is opening," Claudio said.

Kurt shoved open the door to get out. "Shut up, old man."

As soon as Claudio opened his own door, Smoke shimmed and squirmed over his lap and went bounding into the field, barking at things no one else could see. Within a few seconds, the dog was gone.

"Smoke, no!" Jillian yelled after him.

She got out and tried to give chase, but Kurt grabbed her arm. She tried to jerk out of his grasp. He tightened his hold. He had her right at the elbow, so she couldn't maneuver sufficiently enough to break free.

"We need to stick together. I'm quite sure your dog can take care of himself."

He released her, and she didn't run. She glared at the orphanage's duped and disgraced manager. He was right, of course, but she didn't want to admit it. Who knew what was going on? They couldn't risk splitting up if there was any real danger. The wind barraged against her, blowing her hair and making her eyes blur with tears.

"Come on," Claudio said, moving past them. "Time is short."

The trio made their way to the orphanage's entrance. Jillian and Kurt moved at a brisk pace while Claudio limped after them. All the while, the wind bayed like an angry god. Underneath its ululation, Jillian could hear Smoke, barking and howling with it. She hated leaving the dog to fend for himself. He'd been her companion for so long, comforted her at difficult times, known her longer than anyone else in her life save for her folks, who she rarely saw or spoke with anymore. But Kurt was right. Smoke could take care of himself. The dog was a badass. When she'd rescued him, he'd been a scared, frail thing. His previous owners had four teenage boys who used to toss firecrackers at him for their sick amusement. The parents hadn't given a solid shit about the abuse either. And yet, Smoke had persevered. He got himself back up to a healthy weight and became a loving, trustworthy companion.

Smoke would be fine. It was herself she wasn't sure of.

She vowed that when they got to the bottom of whatever was happening now, she'd take him on a long vacation. They'd go to the Poconos and hike the trails, eat overpriced meat and drink cabernet. Once she had her closure, once she knew what happened to Brandon and Bryce, she would take time to focus on herself. Though she hoped with every fiber of her being that Brandon was alive, she feared the absolute worst. She couldn't imagine anyone who disappeared in the middle of the night ever wound up remotely okay.

The wind howled on. Jillian and Kurt reached the front door. She imagined opening it and a carpet of worms spilling out to greet them. How had that even happened? It defied logic and possibly even physics, but if it happened once, it could happen again. Something was very wrong here in Chadds

Ford. There was a putrid stink in the air. She thought she'd imagined it upon getting out of the car, but now she was absolutely certain: the wind carried with it the scent of rot.

While Kurt fiddled with his keys, Jillian turned to see how far behind Claudio had fallen. To her surprise, the old man had limped along quickly enough. He was only a few paces behind them and would catch up any second. Kurt flung open the door. Despite the aggravated climate outside, the inside of St. Luke's was strangely placid.

They entered, one after the other. It was dark inside, save for the blaze in the fireplace, and astonishingly quiet. Where the hell was everybody? Where were all the kids? It couldn't possibly be bedtime already.

Once Claudio was inside, Kurt slammed the door shut. It muffled the wind, but not by much. Somewhere nearby she heard the crack and crash of a fallen branch. She listened for sounds of her dog, but they were swallowed by the wind.

He's fine, she told herself. *He's fine. We're gonna be fine. Dear God, please let everything be fine.*

"Who are these people, Kurt?" someone asked from the shadows.

The voice came from an imposing shape, a tall, broad-shouldered man who nearly filled the door frame across the room.

"Lionel!" Kurt said. "Thank God. Where is everybody?"

"Who are these people, Kurt?" Lionel repeated, a hell of a lot more sternly than before.

"Don't worry about them, okay? You answer to *me,* remember? Where's Myra? I need to speak with her immediately."

"I'm afraid she's busy." Lionel cracked his dirt-smudged knuckles. "Don't you have some paperwork to finish?"

Something clicked in the room behind Jillian. Claudio stepped forward, holding something dark and elongated. The sight of it made her heart sink. "A gun? You didn't say anything about a fucking gun!"

Claudio ignored her. He aimed the weapon square at Lionel. "Now, you listen here, *signore*. You tell us where Myra Jones is, or I put you on the floor, and we'll find her on our own. *La tua scelta.*"

Kurt held up his hands in a peacemaking gesture. "Look, no one's shooting anybody. Let's just…"

He didn't get to say another word. Before anyone could react, Lionel grabbed Kurt by the shirt collar and shoved him into Claudio. The two men stumbled over each other. The gun went off, firing a round into a framed photo on the fireplace. Plinking glass gave way to the massive report. Jillian dropped to her knees. It temporarily deafened her to all but a throbbing sound that could've been an echo of the gunshot or the amplified beat of her heart.

Lionel ignored her to punch out Kurt and then focused on trying to disarm Claudio. He thrust his fist back and delivered a short but powerful blow to Kurt's jaw, making the man drop to his back in a crumpled heap. He then reached for Claudio's wrist. The old man was still clutching the gun but was pinned under the unconscious Kurt and couldn't get enough leverage to turn the weapon on his attacker.

Despite her shouting, Lionel operated as though Jillian wasn't even there. Even in her excited state, she saw the opportunity to use this as an advantage. She scrambled to the fireplace and reached for the sharpest poker she could find. As Lionel wrestled with the aged, but strangely feisty, Claudio, she ran up on him, fire poker raised. He didn't see her coming, and it cost him. The backhanded blow caught him right on the left ear. Though it wasn't enough to knock him out, it sent him reeling long enough for Claudio to hand her the firearm. She didn't like the idea of handling a gun or how quickly this situation was escalating, but this was absolutely the right move.

Maybe there wasn't an actual gate to Hell under this orphanage, but there was some shady shit happening here, and it had caused both her and a lot of others a ton of pain. The police had been no help. Maybe they'd listen to her now, but she and the others had already come so far on their own, she had to see it through. Resolve it on her own. Let the police clean up whatever was left, if anything was left. She hoped she wouldn't have to kill anyone, but she thought she could if she had to, especially if this guy or anyone else tried anything funny.

She pointed the weapon at him. "All right, asshole. I believe my friend here asked you a question."

After Lionel told them everything they needed to know, Kurt dusted himself off. Blood dribbled from his nose and lips. Jillian held the gun on the henchman while Kurt and Claudio tied his wrists and ankles together using curtains they took down from the windows and ripped into strips. All the while, he scowled and informed them they were going to sorely regret this. Jillian's hearing had come back in time to register his threats. Claudio took the gun back from her, and she reclaimed the fire poker. Together, they went to Kurt's office.

Lionel called after them, "These fucking curtains won't hold me forever. I owe you for that fire poker blow, bitch."

She tightened her grip on the metal weapon. Suddenly, it didn't seem like it would be enough, and she found herself wishing she still had the gun.

Kurt pulled a Louisville slugger from on top of the bookshelf and took a practice swing. Claudio's gaze drifted to the bookshelf and his eyes widened. He rushed to it and pulled one of the books off the shelf. His bearded cheeks reddened, and his features twisted as he held up the tome. The title read *The Seven Evil Spirits*.

"This book! Where did you get this?"

Kurt frowned and narrowed his eyes. "I've never seen it before in my life."

Lionel burst into laughter in the other room. The sound sent a chill vibrating through Jillian's nervous system. "You're too late!"

There was a gush of wind and the crash of breaking glass from the newly installed window. What happened next defied not only simple logic but everything Jillian thought she understood about the world. That was the terrifying theme of the day.

Gleaming shards of glass levitated in the air. Its most jagged edges pointed toward the place beside the bookshelf where Kurt stood. Lionel continued to laugh, alternating between guttural guffaws and high-pitched cackles. The glass shards sailed across the office. Jillian screamed, but her voice was soon drowned out by the pain-filled cries of Kurt as the glass impaled him. His face. His throat. One piece popped his eye like an overripe berry. Others stuck into his cheeks and forehead, giving him angry, red gills. The wounds in his neck bled the heaviest, great crimson gouts spurting like muddy water from a sprinkler, soaking his shirt and spattering the floor.

Lionel roared, *"You're all too late!"*

Jillian screamed and pressed herself against Claudio. She gripped his arm with one hand and the fire poker with the other. Kurt slumped and crumpled to the floor, bloody and full of glass. He twitched and gagged. He was alive, but he wouldn't be for long.

This was too much. They were in way over their heads.

Claudio took hold of her wrist. "We must finish this."

When he grabbed her, he'd dropped the book. It lay open, face-up, and she saw a monstrous face drawn on the open page. Everything below the nose had been reduced to shredded gristle. Its eyes were misshapen and misplaced.

"We have to stop the gate from opening," he

added. "To the basement, at once!"

His eyes staring off into nothing, Kurt breathed his last. Claudio released Jillian's arm and left the office.

With her resolve strengthened, she followed.

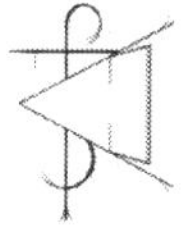

"You're too late!" Lionel called again. "You're all *fucked*."

When Claudio threw open the basement door, he worried the bastard might be right. He'd been too late before. Always belated, always several steps behind those who wished to open these cursed gates. But this time—*this time*—he knew things would be different. He'd had decades to prepare, had gone through the trouble of finding the key—*La chiave del Signore*—with the blood of patron saints, done seemingly endless hours of research and divination. And yet…it appeared the bastard was right.

The stairwell leading into the basement was unfinished. Parts were cinderblock, other parts were just compacted dirt and clay. The stairs themselves were creaky wooden planks, weathered by years of moisture and neglect. Upon entering, Claudio felt very cold. Jillian must have felt it too, because she hissed a breath through her teeth.

Or maybe she'd hissed at the strange light that filled the basement below. The orange and red flames that weren't really flames crawled up and across the cinderblock walls like a living thing. Like the ghost of an exotic plant shown growing through time lapse photography. Tendrils of it wisped and whirled, wrapping around beams and spilling over the dirt floor. The color changed too. First, it was orange and red. Then, yellow and green. Blue and purple. Gray and black. The sound that accompanied the unreal imagery nearly brought his aged heart to a halt. It was a gritty sound, like bones packed in a cement mixer or a million grinding teeth.

"We can't stop now," he said. "We might not be too late."

He wanted to believe himself.

Jillian began to whimper. "What the fuck is down there? *WHAT THE FUCK IS DOWN THERE?*"

He felt for her. Wanted to whimper himself. All the preparation in the world, he never thought he'd really ever get the chance to look into Hell. He couldn't imagine where Jillian's head was at, having only the afternoon to prepare. Still, he went on, and so did she.

The mouth of Hell was a muddy hole in the

basement of Saint Luke's. A half-circle of jagged stones ringed one side of its circumference. On the opposite side, a little girl was on her knees and sobbing. Her hands were tied at the wrists. A middle-aged woman in a black cloak stood behind her, holding a golden dagger to the back of her neck.

"What the fuck?" Jillian muttered.

The woman, who Claudio assumed Myra, turned to sneer at the intruders. Her eyes blazed with a youthful fury. She flexed her grip on the weapon.

"The final sacrifice," Claudio said. "We're *not* too late."

"I beg to differ, old man!" Myra spat.

Claudio looked inside the hole. A large, wooden door, adorned with little more than a simple knob, had been pulled open from its square base in the ruddy earth, and now sat straight up in the air. Steam sizzled on the backside of wood. Shaking, Claudio leaned closer. Something sinewy and lumpy roiled under something milky and membranous beneath the base, like moistened dead skin.

"What is it?" Jillian asked, barely above the awful grinding sound.

"*Colui che aspetta.* The gateway demon. One of the seven evil spirits. It must take the final sacrifice itself for the ritual to be complete."

"No," Myra said. "You're too late, old man.

Even with the blood of the saints, you can't stop—"

Without hesitation, Claudio raised the gun and shot her. He'd waited and studied too damn long and hard to listen to some comic book villain crap from this woman. The slug caught her right above the collar bone. Blood sprayed from the wound and onto the thing in the hole. Like water on a hot pan, the crimson fluid sizzled and steamed when it pattered on the membrane. A gray ragged arm punched through the thick barrier and reached out with jaundiced overgrown fingernails. It blindly clawed at the air while the creature it belonged to moaned like a dying man begging for morphine.

"Get the girl now!" Claudio yelled.

Jillian pushed past him. When she reached the girl, the monstrous arm reached for her. She swung the fire poker. The creature caught it and the metal began to melt in its grip, dripping soupy, gray liquid into the dirt. The creature's ruined face pressed against the membrane now. Even with the film obscuring it, Claudio could see the disproportionate eyes, the mangled lower jaw.

Ignoring the other woman, Jillian abandoned the fire poker, scooped the little girl into her arms, and made her way back to Claudio. Behind her, in the dirt, Myra squirmed, bleeding badly but still alive. Her blood spilled into the hole, almost running toward it like a magnet, mixing with mud and collecting on the fleshy sack. Rags of it were ripping away as the fiend clawed and chewed its way out, feeling around for the blood source. When it found the writhing Myra, its foul claws dug into the flesh of her midsection, opening her stomach and spilling more blood before dragging her, screaming, into the hellish hole.

Claudio's heart skipped a beat. "No..."

Jillian turned and frowned. "What?"

"I should've made sure she was dead. Now, she is the final sacrifice."

"You don't mean…"

"Yes. The gate will fully open."

As soon as he uttered the words, a geyser of blood poured from the hole in defiance of gravity, spraying the cobwebbed ceiling, spraying the floor, spraying the walls. It covered everything, even Claudio, Jillian, and the little girl. The sound was like seawater rushing through a hole in the hull of a ship doomed to sink.

Claudio shoved the gun into Jillian's trembling hands. "Take the girl and go!" he shouted above the deluge.

"What about you?"

He produced the key full of saintly blood from his coat pocket. "I've got a job to finish."

Jillian continued to stare at the scene.

"Partire!"

She nodded and led the girl up the stairs.

Her hand in the tight grip of a stranger's, Annie was hurriedly dragged up the narrow, rickety staircase to the kitchen above. The woman squeezed hard enough to hurt. Annie was lucky her arm wasn't yanked from its socket. Everything was happening so fast. She had no idea who this woman was or where she was being taken. All she knew was she was grateful to be whisked away from that liar Miss Myra and the terrible thing Annie had helped unleash from the door in the ground.

"Come on!" the woman screamed. "Faster!"

By the time they reached the linoleum floor above, the basement below was rumbling, shaking the walls like a diesel truck was parked beneath them. There was no time to consider what that terrible beast was, or to even catch her breath. The woman hauled Annie toward the hallway and into living room, presumably to the front door.

When Annie saw him, she yelped.

In the middle of the floor, Mister Lionel was

down on his knees, his hands tied behind his back. His head was pointed up, staring at something she couldn't see. Although he wasn't actually *looking* at anything. Both of his eyes were now gone. Blood wept from the gored holes in his face like fat, ruby tears.

The man didn't move his head when he spoke. "I can see… I can finally see…"

Thankfully, the woman holding her hand didn't ask him what he supposedly saw as she took Annie across the room to the front door. Annie tried not to look at him as they passed, but she failed. Mister Lionel continued to stare into the middle distance, witnessing a hell Annie hoped she would never see. She almost felt sorry for him. *Almost.*

The woman threw the door open, and beyond the threshold the wind nearly bowled them both over. They pressed on, hopping down the porch steps and onto the front lawn. The front door slammed shut on its own behind them. Annie's long blonde hair whipped around her head, obscuring her vision. When she managed to hold it out of her eyes, she wished she hadn't. She screamed hard.

The woman holding her hand skidded to a halt and pulled her close. *"Jesus Christ!"*

They were surrounded by the undead.

The small, childlike shapes littered the front lawn. They struggled to stay upright against the unnatural breath of Mother Nature, but they did anyway, shuffling and hobbling on uneasy feet. Their heads were down, eyes closed. But Annie knew where they were heading.

Right for the house. Right for them.

Despite the gun in her hand, the woman above her toiled with what to do next. Gasping for breath, she pulled Annie toward the parking lot, where they could see Mister Kurt's car, but that, too, was overrun by shambling juveniles. They seemed to be everywhere, hundreds of them, all converging on the house. Some Annie recognized, many she did not. *I caused this*, she thought.

The woman kicked at the grass. "No, no, no, no! Shit!"

Annie had seen enough. She fought against the woman's grip, wanting to leave her indecisiveness behind and run for her own life. "Let me go!"

But the woman tightened her grip. "Stop that!"

The undead children drew closer. Moaning. Rotting.

Quickly running out of options, the woman spun in the circles until she decided on a direction to take them.

That direction was the woods.

Panic washed over Annie as she was pulled away. *"No! We can't!"*

"Damn it, stop struggling and come on!"

Annie struggled with the woman, but the woman wouldn't let up. Before they reached the tree line near the backyard, Annie dug her heels in the grass and held firm. "I'm not going anywhere with you! I don't even know you!"

Still covered in drying blood, the woman huffed as she glared down at her. "What are you talking about, kid?"

"I. Don't. Know. You. And *you* don't know what's out there."

"*Really?* Are you actually doing this *right now*?" She glanced behind them as the undead slowly but surely followed with a rigid gait.

Annie glared at her defiantly. "Ma'am, I've been taken advantage of *one* too many times lately, and I am not taking another fucking *step* until I know who you are and where you're taking me." She was not one for cursing—in fact, she loathed it—but now was not the time to worry about salty language.

"What's your name, kid?"

"Annie."

"Look, Annie, unless you plan for the both of us to be stuck between the teeth of your peers in the next several seconds, I suggest you stop acting like a goddamn brat and do as I say."

Refusing to let up, Annie crossed her arms and

stood up straight.

The woman continued to glance back and forth. "Fine! My name is Jillian, *okay*? I came to town to look for my missing boyfriend, and instead I found a whole big clusterfuck that we're now both involved in. Look, I don't want to hurt you. Okay? I just want to get us as far away from this place as I can and get us both to safety. Okay? I know you've had a rough night, but it's about to get a hell of a lot worse if we don't get a move on. *Okay?*"

Though she had no reason to trust this stranger, unlike the other adults in her life, Jillian seemed to be telling her the truth. For once, despite her rude demeanor, it was refreshing. She nodded, eyeing the trees as she allowed yet another grown-up to take her somewhere dangerous.

The woods were even darker inside. Despite the power of the wind, it somehow couldn't cut through the trees, nor could the moon bleed in overhead. Add to that their heavy breaths, and the forest was even more unnerving than being out in the open. Now forced to trust Jillian with her life, she allowed the adult to lead her blindly through the dense thicket. She sucked in shuddering breaths, trying to let her mind fly high above, away from the horror. But it remained grounded, below the kitchen, beneath the dirt, beyond the wooden door… So many eyes had watched her as she dug, as Miss Myra, the woman in the black cloak, who held that long, stained, threatening blade, instructed. That was it for her, she had believed, and after what she had witnessed and experienced, both before and after the gate, she had been ready to die. Whatever was rising to the surface was because of *her*, and before Jillian and that old man had saved her, she had accepted her fate. But now, in the depths of these woods, as more of the stiff, lumbering forms revealed themselves through the trees, she wanted more than anything to live.

As soon as Jillian saw the children, she pulled Annie to the nearest open clearing. But the undead, though slow moving, steadily filled the forest floor. Jillian yelped as she tried to dodge them. They continued to reveal themselves, appearing from behind trees, sitting up from the foliage. Cutting them off. Their faces were expressionless. Some had their eyes. Others didn't. Jillian finally let go of Annie's hand and fiddled with the pistol. It was apparent she had never seen one up close, much less held one, because she couldn't seem to handle it properly. She flipped it every which way, holding it sideways as she tried to locate the safety lock.

Annie began to back away, as time was running lean. More children spilled into the dark, taking the spaces between the trees. Shaking hard, Annie continued to walk backwards, knowing Jillian would never figure the weapon out. She turned to run—

—and collided into Grandpa Fred.

Annie shrieked.

The old man was now a ruin of his former self. His throat and shoulders were a galley of bite marks and shredded skin. Old, dark blood had crusted down his flannel shirt. He still had his eyes, but they were vacant and yellow. Stringy threads of green and black goop roped across his face. He angled his head down toward her and moaned.

Annie turned to run back to Jillian—

—and found Edna instead.

She, too, was as dead as her grandpa, and just as eager to take hold of Annie. Out of options, Annie grabbed her ears and screamed with all her heart.

Grandpa Fred reached down with a stiff hand and took hold of her shoulder.

BANG

A gout of cold blood exploded across Annie's face. Grandpa Fred moaned loudly. His grip loosened and then disappeared altogether as his hand fell from her body and dropped to the ground, now separated from his body. Mouth wide with shock, Annie stared at his arm as dark bile oozed from the stump.

"Annie! Move!"

She looked over and saw Jillian aiming the now

functional pistol in her direction. She did as she was told, throwing herself onto the ground as the gun went off again. Above her, Grandpa Fred's chest bloomed with more black blood as the bullet ripped right through him. But it didn't seem to faze him. The elderly man, along with her former best friend continued to stumble toward her.

Jillian stomped forward and shot once more. The old man grew stiff as the back of his head ruptured outward. His eyes still locked onto Annie, he collapsed and joined her on the forest floor.

Edna growled and dropped to her knees next to Annie. She seized Annie's arm and brought it toward her open jaws.

BANG

Unlike Grandpa's head, the front of Edna's face burst open and sprayed over Annie's lap. The undead girl stiffened and then dropped face-down.

Annie sat there, panting, unable to move. She herself grew cold and stiff.

"Annie, are you okay? Talk to me."

She didn't answer. Couldn't.

Jillian popped off a few more gunshots before taking Annie's arm and yanking her up to her feet. "Don't go catatonic on me, kid. Come on, let's go."

Jillian refused to wait around while the rest of the undead trudged after them. Sure, she'd gotten lucky with the few shots she had taken in her crash course on gun play, but not knowing how many bullets remained in the clip would quickly negate the work she had just put in. The forest was quickly filling up, and she had no intention of adding their bodies to the unsteady mass.

After ducking and dodging their way through the dark, they eventually found the moonlight once more. The back country road which circled the property materialized, giving Jillian a flash of hope. The truck she eyed sitting forty feet away turned that flash into a beacon. Taking Annie's hand, Jillian rushed to the parked vehicle, finding it both empty and unlocked. As if things couldn't get better, the keys were even still in the ignition. Relief washed over her. She had zero idea who the truck belonged to, but God bless their stupidity. She helped Annie inside and then started the truck and took off.

It was normally ten minutes to get back to Chadds Ford proper, but putting the gas to the floor put them back into town in the matter of a few deep breaths. Jillian wasn't exactly sure what they would do when they got there. She had left her purse and her cell phone back in Kurt's car, so she had no way of calling the police. She would just have to find the local station and locate that officer she had encountered earlier. How many deputies did he have at his disposal? In a town this small, probably not enough, not for what would be coming their way.

Only...

It was already there.

By the time she exited the country road and entered the small main strip of town, Chadds Ford was already a goner. The undead, both large and small, shuffled awkwardly through the streets and across the sidewalks like packs of stray dogs. Their shadows walked past windows, bumped into parked cars, let the wind nearly push them off their feet. They were everywhere.

Jillian reached across the seat and grasped Annie's shoulder. "Close your eyes, kid. Don't look. Dear God, don't look."

The little girl beside her did no such thing. She stared wide-eyed out the windshield, her gaze fixated at the carnage.

Those who had not joined the undead on their feet remained on the ground as the others dipped hands and faces into their meals. Blood ran freely across the pavement. On their knees, the undead picked through the remains and slowly added their findings to their maw, where they chewed with instinctual fervor. Jillian carefully swerved the truck around them, trying her hardest to not vomit for the second time tonight. Annie wasn't as lucky as she leaned forward and expelled her stomach onto the floorboard.

"My God," Jillian mumbled. "How are they already here?"

They had left the property not even fifteen minutes ago, and the closest town was already gone. The evil was spreading quicker than Jillian could even imagine. At this rate, it would reach Philadelphia within the hour. The math she performed on the fly suggested it would only take a day before the whole state would be gone. What then? Could it be stopped? She immediately thought of Claudio and the horrible thing rising from the gate. She prayed he would stop it in time. She—

Lost in her thoughts, Jillian didn't hear Annie scream as a green sedan barreled down and T-boned them in the middle of an intersection. The passenger door was hit straight-on, and the result threw the truck sideways across the street. Jillian's head lightly rapped the window, but it was enough to produce stars and pain. She bit her tongue, and blood immediately filled her mouth. Still strapped to her seatbelt, Annie threw herself across Jillian's lap. The truck skidded several more feet before finally coming to a stop. Something beneath the hood growled and popped, sending steam billowing from the engine.

Ears ringing and dazed, Jillian opened her eyes and shook her head. Below her, Annie whimpered and held tight to Jillian's leg. "Are…are you okay, hon?"

Annie answered with a nod.

Jillian lifted herself and glanced over the shattered passenger window to the car below. Their front grill was pinned to the side of the truck, rendering the door useless. The man who was driving the vehicle was no longer behind the wheel, as he had exited the windshield and was now lying across the hood. His stomach had caught the ruptured glass and was now shredded wide open, his insides spilling down the side of the car like wet, pink jumper cables.

The undead moaned outside the truck.

"Annie. Get up. Unbuckle yourself. Now!"

The young girl immediately did as she was told. After a quick search, she was unable to locate Claudio's pistol. Fortunately, the police station was just across the street. She shouldered open the driver's door and helped Annie down.

"Are you okay? You're not hurt?"

Annie, shaking hard, shook her head.

"Then run!"

Together, they circled around the ruin of the truck and made a beeline to the police station, weaving between the undead.

They approached the small, one door entrance to the station and hurriedly entered. Jillian slammed the door shut and twisted the lock, already feeling a bit better. But not much. The door itself was mostly glass and would not hold if even a few of the bodies outside were throwing themselves against it. Hopefully they could find that cop she had spoken to earlier. Even if he was it, at least he might have some idea what to do.

"Hello?" she called through the Plexiglas partition. "Officer…whatever your name is? We need help?"

No answer.

"Please! I'm the woman who came in earlier looking for her missing boyfriend. I'm with a little girl from St. Luke's. Some terrible things have happened, and we need some assistance, please!"

Still no answer. The small bullpen beyond the window was dark, save for a few dull computer lights.

Something slammed into the door behind them.

They both shrieked.

Several of the undead had followed them and

now wanted inside, too. Their blood- and goop-covered faces smeared across the glass, their hands pawing and scratching at the see-through barrier. Grabbing Annie, Jillian led her toward the side door and jerked on the handle, finding it locked. They pressed their backs against it.

"Goddamn it!"

The undead continued their assault on the door, rattling it in its frame.

Annie asked. "What now?"

Jillian stuttered a sharp breath, unable to answer.

The door abruptly opened behind them. They both screamed as a pair of arms pulled them backwards.

The cop with the white hair and mustache spun them both around to face him. He pointed his gun like an extension of his finger. "Why did you bring them here?" he shouted. "Why did you lead them to my front door? Now they know I'm here!"

Jillian pushed the gun away from her. "Why did you wait so long to let us in? You heard us out there! We could have died!"

The cop sneered. "Better you two than me."

"You motherfu—"

"Will you two please stop!" Annie yelled.

They both ceased their arguing and stared

down at her.

"Mr. Officer?" she continued. "Will you please help us? We don't want to die. We just want to be led to safety. You once took an oath to serve and protect. Will you please serve and protect us?"

Shaking, the man glared down at the young girl for several seconds before finally letting his pistol fall to his side. "You're right… You're absolutely right. My apologies, young lady." He glanced up at Jillian with remorse in his eyes. "There's a cruiser out back we can take. Let's go."

Jillian nodded. "Thank you."

"Come on." He grabbed his jacket from his chair and a set of keys from the desk and then led them toward the back door. "I wish I had more firearms to hand out, ma'am, but we're a bit short on supplies at the moment. State budgets and whatnot."

Before they reached the back door, a large man lunged out from the dark of the bullpen. Jillian screamed and shielded Annie behind her. The cop tried to back away but was too slow as the other man grasped the back of his head and squeezed. Long fingers pressed into his skull and burrowed deep, immediately breaking skin. It only took a few seconds before the back of the cop's head popped like a ripe fruit, raw brain and bone squeezing between the other man's fingers. The cop dropped the gun and the keys, both clattering to the floor, then a moment later he joined them.

The massive, undead man turned around to face Jillian and Annie.

Lionel stared back at them with his hollow eye sockets. He wheezed out a ragged growl. Blood bubbled over his lips.

Jillian reacted on instinct. She grabbed the nearest rolling chair and ran full force at Lionel. The chair struck him and sent his giant frame tumbling backwards into a computer desk.

"Annie! Now!"

The young girl ran for the back door, and Jillian followed, swiping the pistol and keys from the floor. She didn't bother to check on the cop.

Jillian ran around her and opened the back door herself. The back alley was clear of the undead. They immediately spotted the police cruiser, which they ran to and hopped inside. Jillian put the car in reverse and spun the wheels wildly in the gravel before shooting off down the alleyway and out into the street beyond.

The streets were overrun with the undead. Each one stiffly turned their way as they sped past. Jillian didn't bother to swerve around many of them. She hit them head-on, splattering their rigid bodies across the hood and grill and reduced them all into halves and quarters. By the time they reached the edge of town, the white cruiser had become a crimson mess of brains and blood.

Jillian slowed the cruiser as they approached a stop sign until they came to a complete stop. She let the car idle as she stared off into the inky dark of the highway beyond.

Confused, Annie glanced behind them and then back to Jillian. "What's wrong? Why aren't you driving?"

This isn't right, Jillian thought.

"Jillian…what's wrong? I want to go!"

It's just not right…

Jillian had seen too much, knew too much. So much death. Implausible chaos. She couldn't possibly leave like this. Only they knew, and leaving would make it indescribably worse for everyone. Something had to be done.

For the children. For Brandon.

She glanced over to Annie and shot her a sad smile. "I'm sorry, kid." She then spun the wheel and turned the car back around toward town.

Toward St. Luke's.

Unlike the way they had left it, the front yard to St. Luke's was now empty. Unnervingly so. Annie expected the entire lawn to be teeming with the undead, those who were once her co-habitants of the orphanage, full of life and fun and youthful vigor. She expected Jillian would immediately turn the car back around and they would get the hell out of dodge, but that wasn't the case at all. Instead, the woman who was tasked to keep her safe now parked the police cruiser next to Mister Kurt's car and unlocked the doors. Annie knew this woman had her best interests at heart—she'd shown that much so far—but this was just plain stupid.

Outside the car, the banging beneath the house was thunderous.

"Ma'am, please!" she squealed. "I don't want to go back!"

Jillian's hands shook as she clicked off the safety on the revolver. "Annie, I'm sorry, but we don't have a choice."

"Of course we do! We can run away and never look back!"

Jillian snapped, "And then what, kid? Then what? Hope that the evil coming out of that basement decides to give up and go back home? No harm, no foul? Don't be stupid, Annie. You saw with your own eyes how quickly it's spreading. You and I, we're the only ones who know what's down there."

"Yeah? And?"

"And we have to stop it. Or at least try. If we don't, everything we saw back in town will be everywhere in a matter of days—even hours. Do you want that?"

Annie imagined that very chaos shambling down highways and across bridges, infiltrating every corner of every town and city in America. Blood plastering everything in sight. Innocent people being devoured and then devouring others themselves. Jillian may have been crazy, but she was right.

"No, I don't."

"Good." Jillian popped open her door and stepped outside. "Now come on, while the coast is still clear."

Sick to her stomach, Annie reluctantly exited the vehicle.

The booming within the house before them was even louder outside. Each crash rumbled the foundation, tremoring the cold ground beneath their feet. Jillian didn't have to take Annie's hand. Annie immediately clasped the adult's sweaty palm in her own. Jillian, still jittering, offered her a nervous smile and led them to the front door.

Boom…Boom…Boom

Gun pointed out before her, Jillian entered the

three story house. The electricity wasn't out yet, but it was well on its way, as the lights flickered with each crash. The front room was empty. Framed pictures were now piles of glass on the floor, and anything not bolted down had fallen or had shifted out of place. Loose toys littered the floor. On the far wall, the fire within the hearth still burned, but it was mostly embers.

BOOM…BOOM…BOOM

Annie tensed up as Jillian took her toward the hallway. Something didn't feel right. The air grew denser, and with it came a cloying odor of rot and freshly dug earth. Annie immediately began to sweat. The intense warmth radiating from the doorway before them reminded her of an open oven. She pulled back, but Jillian trudged on and led them into the kitchen.

Jillian stopped just beyond the doorway and gasped.

Annie stepped around her and froze.

BOOM…BOOM…BOOM

The old man from the basement was now lying face-down on the kitchen floor. His prone body was unmoving. What *was* moving, however, was the man who was kneeling down beside him. His back was toward them, but Annie could see the man was yet another member of the undead. He reached down slowly, methodically, and pulled a strip of skin away from a large bite wound on the back of the old man's arm. Bloody skin in hand, the man placed it in his mouth and chewed.

BOOM…BOOM…BOOM

Above her, Jillian growled, "Get away from him!" and blasted off a round from her gun.

Annie winced.

The man's back exploded in a surplus of old, dark blood. His body stiffened, but he barely noticed. Jillian fired another shot, hitting the man in the back of his shoulder. More blood flew as another large hole opened in his body. This time the man reacted. He stood awkwardly, unbalanced, and then slowly turned to face them.

Jillian screamed.

BOOM…BOOM…BOOM

"Brandon…"

The man moaned and faced them both, chewing with a tongueless mouth. While fresh blood dribbled from his lips, his pallid face was a canvas of much older fluids. Browns and greens, reds and purples—all manner of bile and hardened excrement stained his mouth and neck. A large, fat millipede fell from his mouth and skittered away across the floor.

"Oh, my God… Brandon…" Jillian shuddered and began to cry. "What did they do to you?"

Heart hammering, Annie tugged on Jillian's shirt. "Shoot him!"

The adult didn't respond. She continued to weep as the undead man gradually shuffled toward them, moaning.

BOOM…BOOM…BOOM

"Jillian! Shoot him!"

Jillian instead dropped the gun. The weapon clattered on the floor near Annie's feet. "Brandon… No…"

The undead man drew closer.

While Jillian sobbed, her trembling hands holding the side of her face, Annie lunged for the gun. She wasn't exactly weak, but the handgun was much heavier than she expected.

"Brandon, please… Please don't do this."

He moaned in response, her pleads going right through him like her bullets. He was only a few feet away. Overwhelmed with terror, Jillian pressed herself against the wall and screamed.

The man she called Brandon, her undead boyfriend, growled and seized her shoulders.

BOOM…BOOM…BOOM

Bugs cascaded from his snarling jaws as he darted for her throat.

Eyes firmly shut, Jillian recoiled.

BOOM!

In an instant, Brandon's head was blown wide open. Rotten brains burst across the wall beside Jillian, some splashing over her face and chest. Brandon's corpse gradually released her as he dropped to the floor. Jillian gasped and opened her eyes.

Annie, the gun held at arm's length, still had the weapon drawn on the spot where he once stood. Now it was her turn to shake. She shuddered and began to cry, now realizing what she just did.

Wiping her eyes, Jillian walked over and took the gun from her grip. She hugged her hard. "I'm so sorry, hon. I'm so sorry."

"N-next time I-I say shoot," stuttered Annie, "Shoot."

Jillian held Annie's cheeks and pressed their foreheads together.

"Dannazione, fa male!"

They both turned to see the old man rolling over onto his side.

"Claudio!" Jillian rushed to his side. "How…"

"Am I still alive? A miracle at best." He groaned and held the gushing wound on his arm.

BOOM…BOOM…BOOM

A cacophonous roar from the open basement door brought them all back to reality. Jillian stood to face it.

Claudio grasped her leg. "Don't! It's grown too

powerful. We cannot stop it."

Jillian ignored him and strode toward the basement door. Despite the old man trying to hold her back, Annie joined her.

BOOM…BOOM…BOOM

In the dark below, the dirt-covered floor was now gone, replaced by an ocean of swirling, flowing blood. Before her, the steps had all but disappeared as the gateway demon, now fully emerged from the ground, had broken them all beneath the weight of its incredible bulk. Its massive, muscular body filled the base of the bottom of the stairwell. His clawed fists smashed angrily at the walls, the beast trying to bring the house down around him, and they responded by crumbling against it.

BOOM…BOOM…BOOM

Unable to reach the top, the demon glared up to them with its yellow, offset eyes, one large, one tiny, and roared with its shredded, mangled mouth.

Terrified, Annie screamed, "Shoot! Shoot!"

This time Jillian didn't hesitate. She proceeded to unload the pistol upon the demon. The gun blasts deafened Annie, making her ears rings. The beast below roared in anger. But not in pain. By the time the gun clicked empty, Annie realized the gun did nothing to the beast. It bellowed, somehow growing even larger, as it leapt up and pressed its rubbery body against the narrow walls, attempting to widen the pathway to the kitchen. The house cracked and protested, groaning almost as loud as its unearthly destroyer.

Something slid across the floor toward them. Annie glanced down and saw a large metal key at her feet.

"Empty it!" Claudio howled. "*Adesso! Fretta!*"

Annie picked the key up and handed it to Jillian. The woman, as pale as a ghost, popped open the key's lid. The red fluid inside glowed bright. Turning back to the stairs, Jillian tossed a mist of the liquid onto the beast. Its roar became a squeal as the demon writhed in pain. It thrashed against the walls, breaking them to pieces. Smoke filled the small area. Its arms gave out, and the demon went falling backwards and splashed into the frothing pool of blood below. It continued to screech and roll about in pain. Jillian threw more of the red liquid onto it from above. The demon, now too big to move, could do nothing but accept its agony.

"Did we kill it?" Jillian yelled.

Claudio answered, "Not quite."

Both Jillian and Annie went back to the old man and gingerly helped him to his feet. He hissed in pain and held his injured arm. Beneath them, the house shook like an earthquake. "We have slowed him, yes, but the gate remains open! We must close it before it's too late!"

Jillian struggled to hold him up. "I'm not going back down there!"

"Me neither!" added Annie.

"Not necessary." He allowed them to help carry him through the hallway into the living room. Claudio pointed to the fireplace. "We only need to cleanse the house."

Jillian stared at the dwindling fire. "Are you saying—"

"Indeed. Burn the whole thing down. Fire erases everything. A pure, untainted inferno will close that gate. *Adesso e per sempre.*"

"We can't—"

"You can and you must!" he shouted over the rumbling house. "Now!"

Doing as instructed, Jillian raced to the fireplace. Taking a jacket off from the coat hanger nearby, she wrapped it around her hand and used it as a barrier to grab hold of the untouched end of a burning log. She carefully extracted the log and held it out away from her. Eyeing the couch, Jillian made a beeline for the upholstered furniture.

Something dripped onto Annie's head. Then the drip became a steady downpour. Covering her eyes, she glanced up.

The ceiling was raining blood.

Heavier and heavier, the bright liquid showered the room in shimmering red. Before long, Annie's head was drenched.

Claudio yelled, "It's trying to stop you! *Fretta!*"

Completely soaked, Jillian tried to hide the flaming end of the log as the blood attempted to extinguish it. By the time she got to the couch, it was already too saturated to set alight. She jammed the log into the cushions, but nothing happened. Jillian shouted in frustration. "No, no, no!"

Annie couldn't stand by and just watch. She rushed to the fireplace, her feet nearly slipping in the puddles of blood, and grabbed the first log she saw. The blistering wood burned her hands terribly, bringing tears to her eyes. She ripped it from the fire and held it against the coat rack. The remaining coats immediately caught fire. Not letting the blood deter her, she approached the wall and held the log against it. Within seconds, the wallpaper went up in flames. The blaze raced up the wall to the ceiling and spread outward, sizzling the blood.

"Well done, girl!" Claudio shouted.

The couch, despite being soaked, erupted in a ball of fire, starting from underneath and tearing its way up the back rest. Jillian extracted the log and held it against the wall, repeating Annie's process. Before they knew it, the room was an inferno.

Her hands aching, Annie threw her log onto the stairs, and the carpet immediately went up in an orange blaze.

The house responded. A sudden wind ripped through the living room, nearly blowing them off their feet. The flames whipped and spun, but the house was several moments too late. The extra oxygen stoked the fire, spreading it quicker up the steps and through the hallway into the kitchen.

Jillian rushed to Annie and grabbed her hand. "Come on!" Claudio followed close behind as they rushed through the front door, down the porch steps, and out onto the front lawn.

Only now they weren't alone.

Much like the first time they escaped St. Luke's, the front yard was teeming with the undead. Large and small, whole and lacking, they surrounded the house by the hundreds, and the moment Annie and others hit the grass, they slowly moved toward their blood-soaked group. Even if they wanted to, there was nowhere for them to go.

"Jillian!" Annie cried.

"I see them!"

Claudio eyed the undead. *"Dio ci salvi…"*

Inside the orphanage, the conflagration raged like a living creature and swallowed the living room whole. Flames licked the front picture window, roaring as it reduced everything around it to ash.

Jillian cried, "Come on! Come on!"

The dead drew closer, steadily circling them.

Annie gripped her tight. "Jillian!"

"Come on! Do it! *Do it!*"

Claudio put his hands on both of their shoulders and pulled them close. His stoic face gave no emotion.

Flames filled the windows of the upper two levels of the house. Black smoke billowed through the air.

Tears dripped down Jillian's cheeks, as well as Annie's. *Not like this,* Annie thought.

Closer and closer the undead got. They would be enveloped in a matter of moments.

A small boy stumbled toward Annie. Even though his eyes were gone and his chest had been torn wide open, she immediately recognized Bryce. The undead boy moaned and dragged a broken leg behind him.

Above her, Jillian whispered. "Close your eyes, hon."

Annie did.

BOOM!

Something exploded within the house, and a moment later every window erupted. Beneath the house, the gateway demon bellowed a massive roar. The sound rippled the ground below. The roof collapsed into the third floor, turning the upper level into a massive pyre which reached to the night sky. The beast inside cried once more, and another explosion within rocked the foundation.

All around them, the undead combusted. Their stiff bodies froze in place as the flames consumed them. Hundreds of them, lighting the front lawn like the midday sun. An unearthly moan filled the air, swelling like an unhallowed orchestra. The sound rose and rose, claiming their eardrums for its own. Annie grabbed her head and screamed. Then, as if their marionette strings were cut simultaneously, the undead collapsed to the lawn in burning, stinking heaps.

As the house and bodies blackened, Annie glanced up at Jillian. Her eyes full of relief, the woman scanned the area before turning back to Annie. "You did it."

Annie grinned. "We did it."

Claudio dropped to his knees and wept into his hands. "*È finita.* I cannot believe it."

They stayed there for some time, watching the house burn all the way down to the ground. They had to be sure. Annie figured they owed it to the world to do so, even though the world had been less than kind to her.

As the sun began to crest over the trees, Jillian pulled her car over to the side of the country road and put it in park. She hopped out, went around to the passenger side, and carefully helped Claudio from the vehicle. In the backseat, Annie curiously watched them both.

"Are you sure about this?" Jillian asked him.

Claudio closed the door. *"Sì."*

"I just don't understand. Why not come back with us?"

"Because my work is finally done. I have now completed my life's work. I may not have been able to stop the other gates from opening, but I saw to it the very last would never be opened again. And for that, I thank you."

Jillian crossed her arms. "For what?"

Claudio smiled for the first time since they had met. "For giving an old man hope. There will always be evil in this world, *signorina,* but it's people like you who will carry the torch, so to speak, and fight it with all your heart. I applaud you and the little one for being strong and doing what's right."

"We couldn't have done it without you, Claudio."

He waved his hand at her. "*Senza senso!* You've got a gift. Be sure to use it again when the time calls for it."

She pointed at his wounded arm. "What about that? That's not exactly a gift."

He lifted his arm to look. Though they had wrapped it up tight with an old shirt from her backseat, blood continued to drip from his wound. "No, I suppose not."

"Will…will you *turn*?"

The old man seemed lost in thought. "Not sure." He shook his head, lost in his thoughts. "Very…how do you say…apropos."

"I don't understand," she said.

Claudio glanced back up to her and smiled sadly. "Nothing. I must be leaving. I wish you well, *signorina*." He wiggled his fingers to Annie, who waved back, then he turned away and awkwardly hobbled toward the woods. A minute later, the old man disappeared into the trees.

Jillian stood there for a long while, watching him go. She wished she knew where he was going, or what he planned on doing with himself, but she supposed that was between him and God now. She wished him well and hoped he found the peace he was long seeking.

When she got back into the car, Annie leaned forward between the seats. "Where'd he go?"

Jillian sighed, rubbing her eyes. "I don't know, hon. Home maybe?"

"Where's *your* home?"

She turned toward the young girl with a grin. "About a half an hour away. You coming with me?"

Annie's eyes lit up, her youthful vigor finally showing through. "Is there a shower there?"

"Of course."

The little girl sat back and buckled up. "Then what are we waiting for?"

DISSOLVENZA IN NERO

(fade to black)

When Dan Sayles finished his week-long bender, he woke on the floor of his living room surrounded by empty bottles and food wrappers. A thunderstorm rocked the inside of his skull. He felt like someone had stabbed him in the left side with a dirty knife. The hall light was on, but it was clearly daytime. Even with the shades drawn, he could tell. The television played some trashy reality show. At some point, he must have stirred enough to mute the volume. Probably to prevent the colossal headache from worsening.

Good thinking, drunk Dan!

He sat up and braced, expecting a surge of bile that blessedly never came. He found his feet and made himself stand still before trying to walk anywhere. He wobbled a little, but nothing too serious.

More important than anything else, the demonic face he'd glimpsed in the pages of that book had faded from his mind. He still sort of remembered it, but now he recognized it for what it was. Some sketch a cave person had done, likely after eating mushrooms they found in some wooly mammoth shit. A drawing of something imagined. Not something real.

Why it had taken him a week of heavy drinking to dampen the image was another matter entirely. Just one of those things, he supposed.

I'm probably working too hard.

Now, he was ready to move on with his life.

First things first.

He staggered to his shower, braced against the wall and let the hot spray hit his back. When he finished cleaning himself, he decided he should probably see Jillian. He guessed he owed her and her loser boyfriend an apology. He picked up his phone and considered texting or calling. Ultimately, he pocketed the phone and decided to show up in-person. He preferred face-to-face interactions. If she or Brandon told him to get lost, that was fine. It was the effort that counted.

He drove out to her place and parked on the street. The neighborhood seemed quiet. A few kids played street football, but otherwise, no one else was outside. He went to the door, knocked, and waited for the inevitable sound of Smoke barking at him. When he didn't hear it, he cocked his head to the side and chewed his lip. Usually, that dog was very protective and had never gotten used to him.

Dan knocked again, this time a little more firmly. No one answered. No dog barked. One of the kids playing in the street yelled "Blitz." Dan looked over his shoulder and saw someone rush the quarterback. If Jillian didn't answer, maybe he'd walk over and show those kids a thing or two. Then again, he still felt like hell. With his body aches, throbbing head, and burn in his side, he wouldn't be playing any games today. Except, apparently, knock-knock.

He raised his hand to knock again, then shifted his gaze to the doorbell and pressed it instead. The electronic bell rang somewhere beyond the door. He waited again for a response. Something rustled in the grass behind him.

He turned to see Smoke padding through the yard. The dog's head was lowered. He moved slower and less graceful than Dan remembered the dog previously moving. Smoke didn't bark or growl. He only approached.

"Hey, boy. Long time no see." The wolfdog didn't look up. "You okay, puppy?"

Dan stepped off the stoop and met Smoke in the yard. He put out his hand.

"Hey, boy. Remember me? It's your old pal Dan. Your mom around?"

Smoke didn't sniff Dan's hand. He just stood there, hanging his head like it was too heavy for his neck. *What the fuck is wrong with him?*

"Smoke?" he gingerly patted the dog on the head.

Smoke looked up at him. Dan's breath hitched. The dog's irises and pupils were gone. Only the bloodshot whites remained. Smoke's lips curled back, showing his jagged canines. A low growl emitted from his throat.

"What the fuck?" Dan gasped.

Before he could think to do anything else, Smoke jumped on him so hard that he lost his footing. He fell and cracked the back of his head on the concrete stoop. Pain and white spots splashed across his vision. The dog was upon him, heavier than a bag of sand, making it impossible for Dan to take a breath, impossible for him to scream *help me* to those kids in the street.

He thrust his hands in front of Smoke's face to ward off the chomping jaws. The canines pierced the skin between his fingers causing warm blood to patter into his eyes. He tried again to cry out but all that emerged was a high-pitched wheeze. Smoke forced his head through Dan's hands and clamped his jaws around Dan's throat. Dan took fistfuls of the dog's fur, trying to remove the attacking beast to no avail as rabid snarls and gurgling blood gloriously followed Dan into the black.

La fine.

(The End)

Acknowledgements

Wesley would like to thank

Brian Keene, Mary SanGiovanni, Bryan Smith, Ryan Harding, Mike Lombardo, Somer and Jessie Canon, Wile E. Young and Emily Rice, Chris Enterline, Kristopher Triana, Stephen Kozeniewski, Kenzie Jennings, John Wayne Comunale, Joseph Hunt and family, his lovely wife Katie, and of course Lucas Mangum for going on this wild journey with him.

Lucas would like to thank

Wes for embarking on this mad trip with him; Manderson, Scout Tafoya, Ryan Harding, Mona Swan LeSueur, Michael A. Dixon, and Shane McKenzie for indulging his Italian horror vices; Joseph A. Gervasi and Exhumed Films for enabling those vices; Sean Duregger; his readers, his friends, and his family.

The authors would like to thank

Lucio Fulci, Dardano Sacchetti, Elisa Briganti, Giorgio Mariuzzo, Enzo Sciotti, Catriona MacColl, Paolo Malco, Giovanni Frezza, Giovanni De Nava, Ania Pieroni, Tisa Farrow, Ian McCulloch, Richard Johnson, Al Cliver, Auretta Gay, Ramón Bravo, Ottaviano Dell'Acqua, Christopher George, Carlo De Mejo, Antonella Interlenghi, Giovanni Lombardo Radice, Daniela Doria, Fabrizio Jovine, Luca Venantini, Michele Soavi, Adelaide Aste, Janet Agren, Fabio Frizzi, Sergio Salvati, Massimo Antonello Geleng, Franco Rufini, Gino De Rossi, David Warbeck, Cinzia Monreale, Antoine Saint-John, Giampaolo Saccarola, Maria Pia Marsala, Veronica Lazar, Fabrizio De Angelis, that shark, all those maggots and worms, Dickie the dog, that kitten from City of the Living Dead, and everyone and everything that made all those great films so memorable. *Grazie per i ricordi!*

Author bios

Wesley Southard is the Splatterpunk Award-Winning author of *The Betrayed, Closing Costs, One For The Road, Resisting Madness, Slaves to Gravity* (with Somer Canon), *Cruel Summer* and *Where The Devil Waits (*with Mark Steensland), some of which has been translated into Italian, and has had short stories appear in outlets such as *Dig Two Graves vol. II, Midnight in the Pentagram,* and *Clickers Forever: A Tribute to J.F. Gonzalez.* He is a graduate of the Atlanta Institute of Music, and he currently lives in South Central Pennsylvania with his wife and their cavalcade of animals.

www.wesleysouthard.com.

Lucas Mangum is the Splatterpunk Award-Nominated author of *Gods of the Dark Web, Engines of Ruin, Saint Sadist, Mania, Pandemonium* (with Ryan Harding) and *Extinction Peak.* His short stories have appeared in the anthologies *The Big Book of Blasphemy, Boinking Bizarro,* and *V-Wars: Shockwaves.* He cohosts the podcast White Trash Occultism and co-founded the publishing collective Less Than Pulp. He lives in Texas with his family.

www.lucasmangum.com.

Ryan Harding is the 3-time Splatterpunk Award winning author of *Genital Grinder* and cowriter of *Header 3* with Edward Lee, *Reincarnage* and the forthcoming *Reincursion* with Jason Taverner, *Pandemonium* with Lucas Mangum, and *The Night Stockers* with Kristopher Triana. Upcoming projects include a new collection, a splatter western, and a collaboration with Bryan Smith.

Made in the USA
Middletown, DE
07 March 2022

62116048R00123